T5-AFR-169

AN ANDREW MAYHEM THRILLER

GRAVEROBBERS
WANTED
(NO EXPERIENCE NECESSARY)

Also by Jeff Strand from Mundania Press

Mandibles
Available in trade paperback and hardcover.

Graverobbers Wanted (No Experience Necessary)
Book #1 in the Andrew Mayhem series
Available in trade paperback and hardcover.

Single White Psychopath Seeks Same
Book #2 in the Andrew Mayhem series
Available in trade paperback and hardcover.

Casket For Sale (Only Used Once)
Book #3 in the Andrew Mayhem series
Available in trade paperback and hardcover.

AN ANDREW MAYHEM THRILLER

JEFF STRAND

GRAVEROBBERS WANTED

WANTED

(NO EXPERIENCE NECESSARY)

Mundania Press

Graverobbers Wanted (No Experience Necessary)
Copyright © 2000-2005 by Jeff Strand

All rights reserved under the International and Pan-American Copyright Conventions. No part of this book may be reproduced or transmitted in any form or by any means, electronic or mechanical including photocopying, recording, or by any information storage and retrieval system, without permission in writing from the publisher.

This is a work of fiction. Names, characters, places, and incidents either are the product of the author's vividly weird imagination or are used fictitiously, and any resemblance to any actual persons, living or dead, events, or locales is entirely coincidental.

A Mundania Press Production

Mundania Press LLC
6470A Glenway Avenue, #109
Cincinnati, Ohio 45211-5222

To order additional copies of this book, contact:
books@mundania.com
www.mundania.com

Cover Art © 2003 by Darrell King
Composition and Design by Daniel J. Reitz, Sr.
Production And Promotion by Bob Sanders

ISBN: 1-59426-348-5

First Trade Paperback Edition • March 2005
Library Of Congress Catalog Card Number: 2003108293

Printed In The United States of America

10   9   8   7   6   5   4   3   2   1

CHAPTER ONE

"I'm not going to tell you kids again to knock it off! If I have to turn this car around and cancel my stakeout, there'll be no TV for the rest of the *month!*"

"It's July twenty-eighth. The month's almost over," said my daughter Theresa with a grin. She's been alive for eight years, and been a smart-ass for six-and-a-half of them.

"Don't be cute. Now I want you to behave yourselves. I bought you nice new coloring books and crayons, so use them!"

"Can I color on Kyle?" asked Theresa.

"No you may not."

"Even if I stay inside the lines?"

My wife Helen says that Theresa takes after me, and as happens more times than I can count, she's right. That's why I try to let Helen handle as much of the child raising as possible. It's better for society that way.

"I'm not going to tell you again," I warned. Then I used language I shouldn't be using in front of children (at least, children with a tendency to repeat colorful phrases in front of their mother) as I realized that I'd just missed my turn. "Okay, that's it. Tomorrow morning both of you are being shipped off to that munitions factory in darkest Peru."

"I didn't do anything!" Kyle, my six-year-old, protested.

"Then you get to go to the factory where they'll feed you

every few days. Your sister has to scrounge up bugs."

If Helen were around, she'd have said something like "You're only encouraging them." But she wasn't here. This was a very good thing, considering that I was about to dump my children off with my irresponsible friend Roger Tanglen while I went to videotape an adulterous husband in the act. While I'll admit that I'm not always the best judge of what activities Helen will and won't approve of, this seemed like an above-average candidate for the "won't" category.

But there was nothing else I could do. Helen was working at the hospital, and the babysitter canceled at the last second for an emergency appointment with her palm reader. So if I wanted to obtain proof that Jake Ballard was playing sink-the-salami with a woman three cup sizes too large to be his wife, I had to do something with the kids. Roger worked weekend shift as a customer service representative for a small mail-order cheese company and had nothing to do during the week except play Minesweeper on his computer, so he was readily available.

I guess I could have postponed the job, but I desperately needed the money. I don't want to bore you with the details and reduce your opinion of me this early in the narrative, but suffice it to say that there'd recently been an event that involved the expiration of my car insurance, the accidental smashing-into of a very nice automobile, a frantic deal with the owner of the very nice automobile, and a wife who didn't know anything about it.

My kids were quiet for the rest of the drive, which was impressive even though it only lasted another three minutes. I pulled into a parking space in front of Roger's first floor apartment.

"I won't be gone more than an hour," I said.

"Kyle's a pig," Theresa informed me.

"I'm pretty sure he isn't a pig. Now, if you're both good, we'll go out for ice cream when I get done, okay?"

"Hooray!" shouted Kyle.

"I want both of you to avoid acting like monkeys while you're with Roger. He has a boring life and wants to keep it that way."

"Kyle really is a pig, Daddy."

"I am not!" Kyle insisted. I was inclined to agree with

him, since he was probably the thinnest first-grader at Chamber Elementary, but sisterly insults don't require a strong adherence to logic.

"Yes you are. You're a big snorty pig." Theresa made some amazingly skillful snorting sounds at him. Kyle began making snorting sounds back. It was a snorting extravaganza the likes of which I'd never heard.

"If I hear one more snort you can forget about ice cream," I said, raising my voice to what passed for Very Stern Daddy mode. "I have to get going, so please be good."

Theresa's expression turned serious. "I'll be good, Daddy. I was just playing."

"Thank you. That's what Daddy likes to hear. Now give me a kiss."

After dropping them off with Roger, I drove out of the apartment complex and ten minutes later turned onto Webster Street. Webster Street is one of the nicer areas in Chamber, which is one of the nicer towns in Florida. It has about thirty-five thousand people, a couple of decent movie theatres, a bookstore where the owner calls me whenever a new *Flip the Weasel* cartoon collection comes out, nice schools, nice parks, nice restaurants, and a guy who mutters memorable television quotes while wandering the streets giving the finger to unsuspecting motorists. If you're ever looking to relocate, you could do much worse.

As I passed the residence of Mr. Ballard, I noted that the only car in the driveway was a red Pontiac Grand Prix. So the Whoremobile (as Mrs. Ballard lovingly referred to it) hadn't arrived yet, and wouldn't for another fifteen minutes if his mistress kept to her lunch hour tryst schedule.

I drove four more blocks down and parked my car at the end of the street. I'd bought it a few years ago, and it was exactly like the sleek black convertible I'd always wanted in college, except that it was gray, boxy, had a roof that wouldn't convert, a smashed front end, a floor covered with about an inch-thick layer of candy wrappers, and "Wash Me!" written in the dirt on the back windshield.

After scooping up Helen's video camera, I got out of the car and began to jog, cutting through a few backyards until I stood behind the Ballard residence. There were a couple of trees, one of which contained a treehouse that looked like I could bring it crashing to the ground by spitting on it. According to Mrs. Ballard, if I hid in this treehouse I'd have a perfect vantage point of the bedroom window where the escapades were to occur.

I glanced around to make sure nobody was looking, put the camera strap around my neck, and climbed the rickety ladder up into the treehouse. It was well-stocked with comic books, soda cans, and a custom-made Quadriplegic Barbie. Returning my attention to the bedroom window, I looked through the eyepiece of the camcorder and saw that as long as they didn't close the curtain I was indeed going to have a great seat for the show.

About a quarter after twelve I heard a car pull into the driveway. About two minutes after that I saw Mr. Ballard burst into the bedroom with a certain "vicious, backstabbing, silicone-addicted slut" who was already half-naked. I began videotaping, feeling like an amateur pornographer. Not that that's such a bad feeling.

They were on the bed in no time, and decided to make my job even easier by staying on top of the covers. In the amount of time it takes me just to fumble out of my shoes, they were going at it. *Good Lord* were they going at it. The acrobatics involved were stunning, and both of them *had* to be double-jointed. I couldn't believe I was witnessing actual human bodies accomplishing these miracles of flexibility—it was like a combination of performance art and freak show.

I've always been in pretty good physical shape, but this display made me feel woefully inadequate, a sexual doofus. Maybe on the way home I'd pick up some literature on the subject.

The problem is that while I was staring slack-jawed at the astounding feats taking place in the bedroom, I was neglecting other important elements in the situation, such as the three angry-looking guys who were now standing at the bottom of the tree.

"See anything good?" asked one of them.

I was so surprised that I dropped the camera. I let out a cute little noise, something like "Uugghck," as the strap did its best to strangle me. I got things quickly under control, but my upper hand on the situation was effectively shot to hell.

"Hello, gentlemen," I said, leaning out of the treehouse and trying to salvage a bit of dignity in my voice. "This is official business, so I'm afraid I'll have to ask you to leave the area."

The guys shared an amused look. "Which position are they in?" asked the one who'd previously inquired as to whether I was seeing anything good. He looked like he should be named Biff, so that's what I'll call him.

I shrugged. "Hard to say. It changes every few seconds." I had the evidence I needed, so I figured my best plan of action was to climb down and see if I could reason with these guys. Maybe offer them each a copy of the tape, after I added a classy soundtrack.

After I reached the ground, I realized that these guys were much larger seen up close. One of them was kind of skinny (I'll call him Winslow) and I could have possibly taken either of the more athletic guys one at a time, but if I had to fight all three I was in pretty big trouble.

They were all in their late thirties, about the same age as Mr. Ballard, so there was a good chance they were friends of his and not merely concerned citizens. "Okay, okay, you caught me," I said. "You probably think that I'm some kind of—"

Obviously they weren't particularly interested in what I thought they thought I was, because the guy who wasn't Biff or Winslow (let's call him Hector) punched me in the gut. I doubled over and made another uuggchk sound. Biff grabbed me by the shoulders and slammed me against the tree, while Winslow yanked the camera off my neck. He began to swing the strap over his head, lasso-style.

"You guys really ought to give me back the camera and let me go," I warned. "I'm a private investigator for the top law firm in the state. I can sic every lawyer in Chamber and its neighboring communities on your butts."

I was lying, of course. Not only was I not a private investigator for the top law firm in Florida, but I wasn't a private investigator at all. Though I thought it would be cool to be an official, fully licensed detective, at the moment I was nothing more than a friend of a friend of a friend being paid to make a dirty video. And if I didn't get the camera back, I wouldn't even be that.

"Do you want to guess how much that scares us?" asked Winslow, while Hector hit the tree with my body again.

"Ummm...more than getting a mosquito bite, less than total nuclear annihilation?"

Hector bashed me against the tree yet again. I was getting a little sick of that, but didn't know the guy well enough to ask him to quit.

Then Biff punched me in the face, knocking me to the ground. This was substantially less comfortable than being bashed against the tree, and my ability to think up amusing comments temporarily disappeared.

I winced as Winslow swung the camera a couple more times, then let it hit the tree. Fragments of plastic, glass, and videotape sprayed everywhere.

"Ow, crap! A piece got my eye!" Winslow yelped, staggering away with his hands against his face.

"That was my wife's camera!" I shouted.

Biff slapped Winslow hard on the side of the head. "You idiot! We could've sold that thing! What's the matter with you?" He slapped him again, knocking him to his knees.

Hector yanked me to my feet. "We don't want to see your sorry butt around here ever again. You leave Jake alone. He's got enough problems dealing with that frigid wife of his. If we catch you again, we'll twist your legs off with a spoon. Got it?"

While I couldn't envision the actual process of twisting one's legs off with a spoon, I nodded anyway. He punched me in the face once more just to show that he could, and then informed me that I was permitted to leave.

I walked back to my car, lacking a spring in my step or a song in my heart. I'd really needed the money from this job, and not just because of my little uninsured car accident. We weren't going to end up on the streets or anything...Helen was a registered nurse, and her salary took care of most of the bills. But while she was semi-supportive of my decision to quit doing clerical temp work and try to earn money without getting a Real Job, her semi-support wasn't going to last much longer if I continued bringing home little or nothing in the way of actual income.

I returned to Roger's place and rang the doorbell. "Daddy! What happened?" asked Theresa as she opened the door.

"Nothing, sweetheart. Daddy just fell out of a tree."

"Are you okay? Do you need to go see Mommy at the hospital?"

"No, no, I don't think that's a very good idea. All Daddy needs right now is a kiss."

I received kisses from both of my children, as well as a painful hug from Theresa, though I was manly enough not to shriek.

"I'll be out in a second," called Roger from the library, which also functioned as the bathroom.

"No rush, we've got to get going," I said. "I'll hook up with you later." Preferably after my face healed, so he wouldn't be able to give me any grief about coming in fourth in the fight.

"Where's the movie camera?" asked Kyle, after we got back in the car.

"It's all over the place. Don't worry about it. Now who wants ice cream?"

* * *

Helen came in around ten o'clock, while I was sitting in our bedroom reading a horror novel called *Whose Heart is in My Popcorn?* Characterization was a bit thin, but boy could that woman write dismemberments.

"Hi," I said. "How was work?"

"Work was fine," said Helen, remaining in the doorway. She's a small woman, barely five-two, with straight brown hair and a plethora of freckles. With her thick glasses, she has a bookwormish, almost owlish look that in no way reveals the "screwing with me would be a bad, bad idea" attitude that rockets through her soul.

"That's good. My day was fine too."

"I'm happy to hear it. Any special reason for that huge bruise on your face?"

I closed the book. "Oh, did that leave a mark?"

Helen folded her arms over her chest. Damn. Not a good sign. I was going to have to work quickly if I was going to get out of this without seeing The Gaze.

"Sweetheart, normally upon coming home and seeing my loving husband with a huge, ugly bruise on his face, the first thing I would do is rush forward, give you a hug, and ask what I could do to make it better." Helen shifted a bit, and I knew I was going to get The Gaze. I just knew it. "However, I could tell from the second I saw you that you're feeling really guilty about something, and you know darn well you've got a hideous bruise. So what happened?"

"It was nothing, really," I said, then cringed inwardly. Error! Error! A statement like that was a guarantee of receiving The Gaze. I was doomed!

Helen frowned and, yes, fixed me with The Gaze. It was a horrible look, a look that simultaneously said "I know perfectly well that you're lying, Andrew R. Mayhem," and "You're not going to have any degree of sex until you tell me the truth."

"Andrew, what happened?"

"It was just a punch," I said, standing up. "Well, two of them. Nothing to get upset about."

"And what exactly did you do to cause yourself to get punched?"

"Someone got annoyed because I was doing a little videotaping. No big deal. These things happen. And expensive cameras sometimes get broken, too. Can't be helped."

Helen finally left her spot in the doorway and sat down on the bed next to me. "What were you videotaping?"

"Something for a friend. An athletic event."

"Andrew..."

I really wished I could lie to her. Make that, I really wished I could lie to her without getting caught. "I was videotaping a guy cheating on his wife. No big deal."

"Cheating on your wife isn't a big deal?"

Ouch, major point deduction there. "No, no, of course it's a big deal, but my taping it wasn't."

"It was a big deal if you got beat up because of it. What if the guy you were videotaping had chased after you with a shotgun? What then?"

"Believe me, if I'd thought there was any chance of me being chased by a lunatic with a shotgun, or any other large firearm, or even a chainsaw, I wouldn't have done it."

"Don't make jokes," said Helen.

"I wasn't making a joke."

"The chainsaw part was supposed to be a joke. Don't do that. This is serious."

"I'm sleeping on the couch tonight, aren't I?"

Helen sighed. "Andrew, you know I'm trying to be supportive of you while you figure out what you want to do with your life. If you want to form a rock band, or become an actor, or a Hollywood stunt man, or a cartoonist, or an archeologist, or a professional baseball player, or any of the other things you've dumped after two weeks, I'm standing by you. But I don't want you getting involved in stuff like taking illegal videos of people cheating on their spouses! I just don't!"

"Got it. I'm sorry." I looked at the floor and felt suitably ashamed. If I'd gotten inside the treehouse earlier, the guys probably wouldn't have seen me, and none of this would have happened. This was all that stupid babysitter's fault for canceling on me. The next time we hired her the little brat was going to find her unlimited access to Popsicles cut off.

"Good. And now that we've put that behind us, let me make you all better."

CHAPTER TWO

About a week later, Wednesday night, I was sitting in The Blizzard Room with Roger. We sat in the back corner of the coffee shop, discussing such weighty topics as why we bothered to keep coming to the Blizzard Room.

"The coffee isn't all that great," I said, using my fingers to mark the number of negative points being made. "The service is slow and surly. There's a disturbing non-coffee smell in the air. There's not a table in the entire place that doesn't rock when you touch it." I touched the table, causing it to rock. "Why do we come here instead of someplace masculine, like a bar?"

"Because we're both deeply lame human beings." Roger took a sip of his double mocha latte. I've known him since seventh grade, when we regularly sat next to each other in detention. In the years since then we'd alternated between me getting him in trouble and him getting me in trouble. We even roomed together in college, where he majored in psychology and I at various times majored in theatre, art history, creative writing, popular culture, and (on a dare) women's studies.

While I'm tall and of average build, Roger is short and slightly pudgy. His hair started saying *adios, sucker!* around the time he turned twenty-two, and his nose takes up much more than its share of facial surface area. Despite that, he's never had any problems attracting women, not with those sapphire blue, soulful, "awwwww, he's *so* adorable" eyes. I've always been jealous of his eyes. My eyes are kind of a dingy brownish color. It's really not fair. In fact, it looked like Roger's eyes were getting him attention once again. A gorgeous blonde was doing a terrible job pretending that she wasn't staring at us. Roger noticed this and waved to her. She smiled, picked up her coffee, and walked over to our table.

"Mind if I join you?" she asked.

"Not at all," said Roger.

As the woman sat down, Roger stuck out his hand. "Roger Tanglen. This is my friend Andrew Mayhem. He's extremely married."

I shot him a "shut the hell up" look, even though I'm far too married to even consider trying anything. It still would have been nice to see if she'd hit on me, even if I couldn't accept her advances. I hope that doesn't sound too pathetic.

"Pleased to meet you, Roger and Andrew. I'm Jennifer Ashcraft. Mind if I smoke?"

"Of course not. Here, I'll join you," offered Roger, whipping out a pack of cigarettes and offering her one. She took it and let him light it for her with his very cool koala bear lighter. (It's a lighter in the shape of a koala bear, not a lighter used for igniting koala bears. Just wanted to make that clear.)

Jennifer looked to be in her early thirties, with long wavy hair and a face that neither had nor required any makeup. She wore jeans and a black blouse that fit *very* tightly and seemed designed to send the message "Hey, everyone, we've got nudity under here!"

"You two look like nice, strong men," she said, glancing around to see if anyone was listening. "Would you say you consider yourselves open to new experiences?"

"Yes," said Roger, too quickly.

She stared me right in the eye. "And you?"

I made a play of scratching my forehead so that my wedding ring was blatantly visible, in case she'd missed Roger's "extremely married" comment. "Uh, yeah, sometimes."

"Good." She opened her pocketbook and removed an envelope.

"Inside this envelope is five hundred dollars. What I'm going to ask is very unusual, and you may not want to do it. If you decide not to accept, the five hundred dollars is for you to forget all about me. Deal?"

"Sounds great," I said. "I'll just pretend you were my algebra lessons in high school."

Roger glared at me as if my sparkling wit might scare her off. "What do you want us to do?"

She leaned forward confidentially. "I want you to dig up my husband's grave."

Roger and I simultaneously leaned forward as well. "I beg your pardon?" I asked.

"My husband was buried last night, and I want you to dig up the coffin."

It was clear from Roger's expression that he considered this task quite a bit less appealing than wild kinky sex. "You're kidding, right?"

She shook her head. "I'm completely serious."

"Is this the kind of thing you usually ask people in coffee shops?" I inquired. "Are you sure you didn't walk in here by mistake thinking it was Maude and Vinny's Discount Graverobbing Emporium?"

"I told you it was unusual."

"And you were damn right."

"Is this a no?"

I hesitated. "It's kind of a no, but it's the sort of no where I acknowledge that you haven't discussed payment yet. I seem to have left my exhumation price list at home."

"Twenty thousand dollars."

Roger and I glanced at each other. That was incredible money for what basically amounted to an evening of illegal manual labor. It would certainly buy Helen a new video camera and pay off the car damages...

No, no, what was I thinking? This was graverobbing! This was ghoulish behavior! This was sick, sick, sick! This could put me in jail, in an asylum, or on a sleazy daytime talk show. The best thing—no, the *only* thing—to do was tell Jennifer we were flattered she'd thought of us to fulfill her disinterment needs, but that we had to pass.

"Twenty thousand cash?" I asked.

"Of course."

"Answer this important question: Do you want your husband dug up for some sort of unholy ritual? Because I don't do unholy rituals."

Jennifer smiled. "Don't worry, there's no witchcraft involved."

"And I don't do college-style pranks, either. If you want him dug up to leave in the passenger seat of your mother-in-law's car, find somebody else."

"I don't know, that might be kind of funny," said Roger. "If I had a mother-in-law."

"Shut up, Roger."

"It's nothing like that," said Jennifer. "The body will never leave the coffin."

"Why, then? If you don't mind my saying so, you don't look all that upset for somebody whose husband just passed away."

"You're very perceptive."

"Well, I have to warn you that after what happened to me last week I'm a little burned out on the whole pissed-off spouse thing," I said. "So tell me why you want this done."

Jennifer gave a casual shrug. "He had a key with him when he was buried. I want the key. Simple as that."

I guess that was quite a bit less weird than other possible reasons for wanting her husband dug up, though the idea still wasn't especially thrilling. "Where is it, in his pocket?"

"Maybe. It could be anywhere. It could be in his mouth, for all I know."

"In his *mouth*? You want us to reach inside a corpse's mouth? And maybe even touch a dead tongue? Have you taken hygiene into consideration?"

"Are you turning down the job?"

"I still haven't said that." I looked at Roger to see if *he* had said that. He hadn't. He was just sitting there looking confused. "How long do you think it takes a dead tongue to dry out?" I asked.

"I have no idea. Now do you want the job or not?"

"I have a couple thousand more questions first. Such as, I'm not an expert in the field, but aren't caskets meant to be permanently sealed? Wouldn't I need to bring along a jackhammer or something?"

"Cheap pine box. Shallow grave. Well-hidden area. A park, actually."

I stared at her for a long moment. "Not to be rude, but I find that a little disconcerting."

"I didn't murder my husband."

"I never would have dreamed otherwise. How did he die?"

"Suicide. And I'd rather not discuss it."

"Fair enough. May I ask why he's lying in a cheap pine box in a shallow grave in a well-hidden area of a park rather than a state-approved casket in a designated graveyard burial site?"

"I'd rather not discuss that, either."

"Okay, how about an easier question. Why did you pick us?"

Jennifer smiled. "I've done my research." She glanced at her wristwatch and sighed. "Listen, I know men hate having to make a commitment, but I'm going to need one right now. Do you want the job?"

Twenty thousand dollars. Well, ten thousand for me. Plus the chance to add something new to my resume. But in terms of eliciting Helen's fury, it had the potential of making the videotaping debacle look like passing out toys to doe-eyed orphans at Christmas.

And yeah, I really needed the money, but spending time in jail for graverobbing would really look bad on a job application.

Ah, screw it. What's life without risk?

"What do you think?" I asked Roger. "It would pay for that trip to Las Vegas you've been dreaming about."

"Ummm...all right." Roger was never big on the concept of independent thought.

"Okay, Jennifer, you've got yourself a pair of graverobbers."

* * *

Helen was working night shift, and the kids spent every Wednesday night during the summer with Helen's parents. I love my in-laws and they tolerate me, but sending the kids over there on a weekly basis was most certainly not my idea. Have you ever tried to discipline children who've been allowed to stay up as late as they want and do whatever they want and whose blood sugar invariably tests six times over the legal definition of "wired?" It doesn't work.

However, not having my wife or kids around meant that I wouldn't have to be home until 6 A.M. Roger and I got in Jennifer's sleek silver sedan and went for a forty-five minute drive, during which she kept the radio volume loud and was unresponsive to our questions.

We ended up in Fleet Park, which is a decent little place located up north, in an area generally known as "way the hell out in the boondocks." Jennifer stopped her car in front of the closed gate and shut off the engine.

"So, are you boys ready?" She was trying to maintain the casual attitude she'd had in the Blizzard Room, but it was starting to falter. Probably had a little to do with the whole digging up her dead husband thing.

I have to admit, I was feeling a bit queasy myself. "I guess so."

She reached down and pulled the trunk release lever, then handed me a folded piece of paper. "You'll find shovels, lanterns, working gloves, and beer in the back. These instructions will show you how to find where he was buried. It's about a mile away, and you'll have to cross through some thick brush. Oh, and there's also a snakebite kit in the cooler, just in case."

"That's very thoughtful," Roger said. "Aren't you coming with us?"

"If I didn't have a problem being near my husband's corpse, I wouldn't have hired you two." She handed Roger a cellular phone. "My beeper number is written on the instructions. Page me when you're done, and I'll be back to pick you up. Now go dig him up, get the key, rebury the grave just as you found it, and come back here. Then you'll get your money."

* * *

We climbed over the gate with no problem and then we were on a dirt path most of the time, so the walk wasn't so bad, except for the fact that Roger made me carry the cooler. After we had to step off the path and walk through moist brush, the fear of disturbing one of the numerous varieties of Florida snakes made things a little less pleasant, but we hurried through without encountering anything more fearsome than an armadillo. Though to be honest, the armadillo scared the hell out of us.

The grave was in a small clearing. Though the site wasn't marked with anything helpful like a sign reading "Dead Guy Below," the freshly turned dirt made it obvious that we were in the right place.

I set down the cooler and sighed. "Well, Roger, this is our last chance to wimp out. We're graverobbing for a woman who probably murdered her husband. Think it's worth the money?"

"I don't know. Let's not even think about it. Let's just dig."

* * *

The dirt wasn't difficult to move, and the digging went fairly quickly. About half an hour later, at approximately the stroke of midnight, we'd unearthed an area about two feet deep. Roger leaned against a tree, finishing a beer as he took his fourth break for the evening. He put the empty can back in the cooler. We may violate burial sites, but damn it, we don't litter.

"And so resumes the twenty-third annual Fleet Park Graverobbing Competition," Roger announced, using the handle of his shovel like a microphone. "It looks like our champion, Andrew Mayhem, is currently leading in the dirt removal process, but can he sustain such an incredible pace?"

"You're pretty cheerful for somebody digging up a coffin," I muttered. "Correction, you're pretty cheerful for somebody sitting on his lazy butt watching *me* dig up a coffin."

"I'm not sitting, I'm standing."

"Shut up. You've been spending too much time around my daughter. Get in here and help me dig so we can get this over with. You may not be aware of this little tidbit of information, but if we get caught we're screwed."

I pushed down on the shovel, and heard a dull *thud* sound. "And he strikes casket!" Roger broadcast. "The crowd goes wild!" He mimicked a crowd going wild as I crouched down and began to push dirt away with my hands.

"Who the hell would drag a heavy coffin all the way out here?" I wondered aloud. "Why not just bury him in a garbage bag or something?"

"That would be disrespectful," Roger pointed out.

In a couple of minutes, I'd exposed half of the coffin lid. The only thing holding it closed was a padlock, which wasn't going to withstand a good smack with my shovel. I lifted the shovel to do just that, when Roger suddenly tensed.

"Did you hear that?"

"What?"

"I think somebody's coming! Hide!"

Roger hurriedly pressed himself against the tree, while I got down on my stomach and hid from sight in the grave. It occurred to me that if this was the police, and they found me lying facedown on a coffin at midnight, I'd probably be going away for a long, long time.

We waited.

Silence.

A couple of minutes passed.

"Maybe I was wrong," said Roger, stepping away from the tree.

I stood back up, brushing off my shirt, and gave him what I deemed to be a suitably dirty look. "Just for that, you're the one searching the corpse for the key. Put on the gloves."

"Let me give that idea full consideration before I reject it," said Roger. He pretended to think for a moment. "Okay, now I've rejected it."

"If we're dividing the money equally, we should divide the duties equally. And since I've done about seven-eighths of the digging, I think it's only fair that you should have to reach into a corpse mouth if it becomes necessary."

Roger shook his head. "Weren't you an archaeology major for a couple weeks? You should have no problem handling dead things."

"I'll flip you for it," I said, taking a quarter out of my pocket. "Call it in the air." I flipped the coin into the air.

"Heads."

I caught it. "Tails," I lied.

"You're lying."

"No I'm not," I lied again.

"Rock, Paper, Scissors," Roger suggested. "It's the only fair way."

"Oh, yeah, real fair. Like I haven't seen you make your selection juuuuuuuust a bit late before."

"How about we both search together?"

"Sure. Why don't we call in some friends, make a group project out of it?"

I picked up the shovel, lifted it above the padlock, and brought it down as hard as I could. There was a loud clang as the padlock broke.

"Now," I said, "I'm going to open this coffin, and one of us is going to have to get the key. I'll make you a deal. I'll get the key if you mow my—"

A bullet fired upward through the lid of the coffin, nearly grazing my ear. With a surprised yelp I leapt out of the grave as two more gunshots were fired from within the coffin, splintering the lid.

Roger dove for cover. "What the *hell*?!?"

Then there was a loud screaming. It sounded like attempts at words, but they were completely incoherent. As I scrambled out of the way of any more potential shots, whomever was inside began to pound on the lid.

Another gunshot.

More screaming.

And then I heard the lid fly open.

CHAPTER THREE

Michael Ashcraft—if this was him—sat up with the loudest shriek yet. He looked about thirty, with black hair that stuck out like a fright wig. His eyes were open wide, as he swung the revolver around wildly. He squeezed off another shot, but was obviously just firing at random, not trying to hit anything.

"Calm down! You're going to be all right!" I assured him, feeling oh-so incredibly stupid as I said it.

Michael's screams stopped and he began writhing back and forth, whimpering. Being buried alive is obviously not conducive to good mental health. Roger and I remained motionless for a long moment, unable to do anything but watch.

Finally I spoke up. "Michael, can you hear me?"

His head began to jerk violently from side to side as he began babbling gibberish. He slammed the barrel of the revolver against the side of his head, but I couldn't tell if it was a suicidal impulse or an insane reflex.

"Listen to me, Michael," I said. "We're here to help you."

He continued bashing the revolver against his skull. I flinched with each blow, but kept my voice calm. "Michael, can you understand what I'm saying? Stop beating the shit out of yourself if you can understand what I'm saying."

Michael dropped the revolver. Blood trickled from the lacerations he'd given himself. He began making a sound that was either laughter or sobbing—I couldn't tell.

He looked at me. That is, he turned his head toward me, though his eyes remained wild and unfocused.

"Who did this to you?" I demanded.

He resumed shrieking.

"Michael, who did this to you?" I repeated, even though I could barely hear myself over his screams. He continued like that for another thirty seconds or so, then died down and began whimpering again.

"We need to get out of here," Roger whispered.

"We can't just leave him like this," I insisted. "You go get Jennifer, I'll stay here and see if I can get through to him."

"Think he has any more bullets in that gun?"

Michael lifted his hands and began to rub his eyes. I could see that his fingers were raw and bloody, the nails cracked, and a quick glance at the bottom of the coffin lid revealed that it was covered with deep scratches that hadn't even come close to breaking through. Once again he started in with those nerve-shattering screams.

Then, without warning, he curled his fingers into claws and ripped out his own eyes.

"*Jesus!*" Roger gasped.

My stomach gave a horrible lurch as I jumped up and rushed over to the grave. Michael's head lolled back, bloody sockets glistening, and he almost looked as if he were going to smile. Then he collapsed.

I could barely bring myself to touch him for fear that he might spring back to life, grabbing for my throat, but I worked up the courage to reach down to his wrist and check for a pulse. There was none. His heart probably gave out.

Roger's hand was pressed tightly over his mouth and I actually expected him to burst into tears. He just sat there, trembling.

"He's dead," I told him.

Roger gave an almost imperceptible nod.

"What do you think we should do?" I asked.

"Kill Jennifer."

"I'm serious." I really needed something to drink. I walked over to the cooler and grabbed a beer. My motor skills weren't at their best, and it took me three tries to open it. I took a long gulp, draining most of the can. "Should we ditch Jennifer and call the cops?"

Roger shrugged.

"We need to decide something. Now, if we call the police, we're going to have some big-time explaining to do. And if we tell them what really happened, even if they don't accuse us of trying to kill him we're still in serious trouble."

"We'll have to lie to them."

"And say what? That we just happened to be passing through the park with our digging supplies when we heard a lunatic screaming underground and decided to give him a helping hand?"

"We could say...I don't know what we could say. Leave me to my nervous breakdown, okay?"

I cracked my knuckles. "We need to cover this up, literally. We need to rebury him. And then find out for ourselves what the hell is going on."

"We know what's going on! That freaky chick buried her husband alive!"

"Maybe. But why would she have us dig him up?"

"She probably thought he'd be dead by now."

I shook my head. "Why would she need us to get the key if she was the one who buried him? It doesn't make any sense."

"There may not even be a key! This whole thing could have been an assassination attempt on us!"

"Oh, sure. I know if I wanted to kill somebody there's no better way to do it than hire him to dig up a coffin holding an insane guy packing heat. C'mon, Roger, we have to be logical."

"I'm sorry, it's just that my sense of logic gets messed up when I watch somebody rip out his freakin' eyeballs! Jesus Christ! Can you imagine what it's gotta be like to be buried alive like that?"

I was trying not to. I closed my eyes for a few seconds to clear my thoughts, and then took a deep breath. Oxygen was usually beneficial in situations like these. "Okay, the first thing we have to do is search the body."

"*You* search the body."

"Fine. I'll search the body. You keep an eye out for anybody who might be coming to investigate."

I took another deep breath, then jumped down into the foot of the coffin. I tried to avoid looking at Michael's ruined face, but I didn't have anything to cover it with except dirt, and throwing dirt on the poor guy's face just seemed wrong.

The first thing I did was pick up the revolver and set it outside of the grave. What possible reason could he have for holding a gun? I tried to envision a scenario in which he'd been trying to kill somebody, who'd buried him alive in self-defense, but couldn't.

Okay, that wasn't important now. I needed to find that key, if it existed. I knelt down, knees wobbling a bit, and began to pat Michael's jeans pockets. The left pocket felt empty. The right pocket had something in it. It didn't feel like a key, but it could be a clue.

I slipped my fingers inside the pocket, still unable to shake the eerie feeling that Michael could lurch at me at any moment. With my other hand I checked his pulse again to be sure. Still dead.

I got a hold of what was inside his pocket. A piece of paper. I pulled it out and saw that it was the best kind of paper: Cash. A twenty dollar bill. A perfectly normal thing to have in his pocket. I shoved it back inside, not wanting to steal anything from the dead that wasn't absolutely necessary. Yeah, yeah, I know that defiling a grave is much worse for the ol' karma than stealing twenty bucks, but I didn't want to push it.

Slowly, I unzipped his jacket, thankful that no blood had spilled anywhere I needed to touch. I opened it and checked each of the inside pockets, finding a stack of about ten business cards held together with a brass clip. In oozing red letters were the words "Ghoulish Delights. Michael Ashcraft, director," along with an address and phone number. I pocketed the cards, and then closed his jacket.

I grabbed hold of Michael by the waist and rolled him over. His neck made a sickening sort of cracking sound as something twisted that shouldn't have.

Once Michael was on his stomach, I patted his back pockets and found nothing, not even a wallet. Damn. With all the pockets searched, I was going to have to move on to less appealing possibilities.

But not his mouth yet.

I stood up. "I need your help," I told Roger. "I'm going to lift him up, and you look to see if the key is lying underneath him."

Roger walked over and crouched down next to the edge of the grave. I grabbed the top of Michael's jeans and grunted as I lifted him up, his body doubling over at the waist.

"Nothing there," said Roger.

I gently lowered Michael, and then sighed. "I don't know what to do. I'm not going to strip the guy naked to find this stupid key."

"Good. Let's get out of here," Roger suggested.

"Not quite yet." I bent down again and pulled up the left leg of Michael's jeans, exposing his white tube sock. Nothing hidden there. I untied his tennis shoe, set it aside, and removed his sock. Still nothing except for some blatant evidence that toenail hygiene had not been a major part of Michael's life.

I removed his other shoe, and something dropped out.

A tiny silver key.

"All right!" I said, picking it up. "Now let's rebury him and get out of here."

I shoved the key into my pocket and climbed out of the grave. With my foot I shut the lid of the coffin. It didn't close all the way, but Michael was just going to have to deal with it. Silently, Roger and I began to shovel the dirt back into the grave.

* * *

Jennifer's car was waiting at the gate, and she hurriedly got out as we approached. "Did you get it?" she called out.

"We'll tell you all about it after we put this stuff back in your trunk," I said.

"Yes or no, did you get it?"

"Hey, we're just a pair of graverobbers trying to relax after a hard night at the office, give us a break. Do you have the money?"

"Of course. Do you have the key?"

"By 'the key,' you would be referring to a small silver object, maybe an inch and a half long, three triangular serrations on the end, smells heavily of foot odor, right?"

"That's the one," said Jennifer, obviously starting to lose her patience.

"I've got it, but I want some answers first," I told her.

"How did your husband die?"

"I told you. Suicide. He blew his brains out, or did you not notice?"

"Is that so? Then why was his head lacking a bullet hole for the aforementioned brains to exit from?"

She frowned. "What are you talking about?"

"I'm saying that he wasn't shot."

"That's ridiculous. Of course he was!"

"Jennifer, sweetie, we just dug up his coffin. I saw his body. His head was intact. He didn't shoot himself. Now why don't you explain to me what really happened, and I'll decide if you deserve the key."

Jennifer chuckled without humor. "I have to say, you're a much better human being than I expected. I did plenty of research, and the impression I got was that you'd do anything for money except get a real job."

"What? Who told you that?"

"None of your business."

"Well, that's wrong," I insisted. "I didn't dig up your husband because I'm some money-grubbing jerk! I did it to keep my wife from finding out that I had to pay off the guy I hit without insurance! That's not greed, that's an honorable motive!"

"What did they say about me?" asked Roger.

"Quiet, both of you," said Jennifer. "Now what do you mean, there was no bullet hole? Then how did he die?"

I folded my arms in front of my chest and spoke slowly, milking every bit of dramatic impact I could. "Until shortly after midnight, he wasn't dead. Your husband was buried alive."

Jennifer's expression of shock certainly looked genuine. "He *what?*"

"He was alive, he'd gone completely insane, and he had a gun. He didn't kill himself with a bullet to the head; he ripped his eyes out and probably had a heart attack. So I'd like a teeny tiny little bit of explanation."

Jennifer looked as if she were going to be sick. "Oh, God...I need my inhaler." She opened her purse and fished around inside it for a moment.

But she didn't take out an inhaler. She took out a pistol.

"I don't have time for this," she said. "Give me the key so

I can give you your money!"

It was the first time I'd ever had a gun pointed at me, if you don't count Michael firing through the coffin lid, and I'm pleased to report that I handled myself very bravely, in that I didn't wet or soil myself. But the feeling rushed out of my legs and for a second I thought I was going to keel over.

"Drop it!" shouted Roger, taking out Michael's revolver and aiming it at Jennifer. Her eyes darted toward him, but she kept her own gun pointed at me.

"Oh, give it up," said Jennifer. "I don't believe for a second that you'll kill me."

Roger shrugged. "Probably not. But I might try and shoot the gun out of your hand, and my aim sucks."

"He's not kidding," I said. Actually, Michael had used up the last of the bullets during his little shooting spree, but I certainly wasn't going to tell that to Jennifer.

Suddenly Jennifer gasped as a bit of blood spattered onto her face. An arrow protruded from her left shoulder. She let her purse fall to the ground and stumbled forward a couple of steps as Roger and I spun around to see where the arrow had come from. Whoever had fired it was hiding amid some trees near the gate.

Another arrow shot out of the darkness, striking Roger in the upper thigh and plunging deep. He let out a cry of pain and tried to make it to the sedan, but within a few seconds another arrow got him in the back. He went down.

I rushed toward a large tree close to the source of the arrows, trying desperately to reach it before I got pierced. An arrow sailed past my leg, missing by inches. After I made it to the tree, which provided sufficient cover as long as the assailant didn't change his or her position, I glanced back at Roger. He lay on the ground, unmoving, while Jennifer threw open the car door and got inside.

A moment later she slammed her fist against the steering wheel in frustration, and I realized that her keys were in the fallen purse. She got back out of the car, rested her right arm on the roof, and fired four shots into the darkness. I didn't hear any sound to indicate that she'd hit anyone.

For a full minute Jennifer and I didn't budge. I could see that Roger was still breathing, though he didn't appear to be conscious. I listened for footsteps, but heard none.

"Okay, Robin Hood, the game's over!" I shouted. "Come out and show yourself!"

Some footsteps began to approach, and they couldn't be more than ten feet away. I figured the person was out of arrows, but I didn't want to test that theory by revealing myself.

"Listen to me," I said. "I'm just the hired help, and I'm perfectly willing to talk this out."

There was no response except for the footsteps getting even closer until it was obvious that the person was on the other side of the tree. The idea that I might be slightly screwed occurred to me, but I tried not to dwell on it.

Okay, I had to do something besides stand there. If the Mad Archer did have more arrows, it wouldn't be difficult to get me into the line of sight and fire. So what I needed to do was leap out and get the element of surprise on my side.

I leapt out and was promptly hit in the side of the head by a metal chain, which surprised me. I would have reflected upon how much it hurt, but I was only conscious for a couple of seconds afterward.

CHAPTER FOUR

I put my serious drinking days behind me after I got married, but in college I'd found myself awakening in the occasional weird location. The meat display at a grocery store springs to mind, not to mention seven-and-a-half toilet stalls (the Morning of the Urinal was not one of my finer moments).

However, no matter how intoxicated I was on any given night, I'd never before woke up in a situation as unappealing as being tied to a chair with a burlap sack over my head, which is where I was now. My arms were tied behind my back with a thick, itchy rope, and the sack effectively prevented me from seeing any of my surroundings.

"Anyone here?" I asked after struggling with the rope for a few seconds.

No answer. Behind me I thought I could hear whispering, but it was so faint that I could neither make out words, nor a voice.

"Hey, it's me, the guy tied to the chair," I called out. "Somebody wanna talk to me?"

Silence.

"Come on, people, let's get a little verbal communication going here," I said, doing a miraculous job of keeping the terror out of my voice. "My wife gets a really stinky attitude when I let somebody besides her tie me up, so we need to get this over with. Where's Roger?"

"He's fine," Jennifer replied. Her voice was coming from at least twenty feet away, and she'd obviously been doing a lot of crying. "Andrew, listen to me. You need to forget about everything that's happened tonight."

"You've gotta be kidding! I'm going to have a phobia of digging up coffins for the rest of my natural life!"

"I'm serious! If you want to live, you can't go to the police! You have to pretend that you never met me, and that this never happened."

"Let me talk to Roger, make sure he's really okay, and maybe we'll have a deal."

Jennifer began to sob, a sound that was quickly muffled. The next sound I heard was that of footsteps walking slowly toward me. Each footstep was accompanied by a creaking sound, as if from wooden floorboards.

Cold sweat ran down my sides as the person stopped directly behind me. There was dead silence for a long moment, during which I held my breath and squeezed my eyes tightly shut, half expecting a bullet to explode through the back of my head.

Something struck me. Not a bullet, a fist. My head jerked forward from the blow, but it wasn't a punch meant to do real damage. Then an open palm slapped my right ear, hard.

I didn't say anything as I nervously awaited the next strike, but it didn't come. Instead, I felt the tip of a knife blade slide underneath the burlap and scrape gently across my throat, not hard enough to break the skin but certainly hard enough to earn my frightened attention.

"I need to know that he's okay," I said.

The blade swirled around in a figure-eight, and then was removed. The person didn't step away.

"This would be a lot less awkward if you would say something. I thought people like you always had those voice disguiser gizmos."

No response.

"Look, I assure you that your whole intimidation thing has been a rousing success! I'm scared! I'll play along with your little game to keep you from slamming that knife through my neck! But you've got to give me some kind of proof that Roger is still alive."

I let out a grunt of pain as my captor punched me in the

face.

"That wasn't proof," I explained.

Another punch, not entirely unexpected. I decided to shut up and let things run their natural course.

Whoever it was stood in front of me, motionless. I could hear nothing but a very soft breathing and Jennifer's muffled crying in the background. Finally, after about a minute, the person walked back to her.

Jennifer's sobs could suddenly be more easily heard—clearly she'd been ungagged. "Please, Andrew," she begged. "You have to promise that you won't involve the police."

I had to fight tears of my own as I realized that Roger was probably dead. I mean, was I really supposed to believe that I could just say "Scout's Honor" and be released? Even if my captor really did intend to let me go, nobody could be stupid enough to trust that I would simply return to my everyday life as if nothing had happened, not without proof that Roger was still alive.

"Okay, listen, Mystery Guest, you want the key, right? I'll give you the key. It's right here in my pocket. I don't want it. Take it."

I thought I heard a snort of laughter.

"Okay, so, you probably already took the key. I'm sort of stuck working with nothing but context clues here, so cut me some slack. If you've got the key, there's no reason to keep Roger. I don't know who you are and I don't care, so just free us and go unlock whatever it is you want to unlock!"

"Andrew, be quiet!" shouted Jennifer. "I have to read you a message. Pay attention. It says 'Your friend is alive, and if you ever want to see him again you won't go to the police. If you so much as look at a cop, believe me he will die and he will die slowly. Do you understand?'"

"Yes, I understand," I said.

I listened to the scratchings of pencil on paper for a few seconds, and then Jennifer began to read again. "'Do not test me, or your friend will end up like'...*oh God no...!*"

Jennifer let out a shriek of terror, which was cut off by the sound of a knife slamming into flesh. I'd never heard that sound before, but there was no mistaking it for anything other than what it was. Jennifer began making gasping and gurgling noises as the knife fell again and again.

After the final plunge of the knife, the room fell silent except for the sound of dripping. My ears were ringing and my fists were clenched so tightly together that my fingernails were digging into the skin.

Then the killer began to walk toward me again.

I was so frightened I couldn't even blurt out a promise to keep quiet. The knife slid back underneath the burlap and moved across my throat the same way as before, this time slick with warm blood. A drop ran down my chest. I sucked in a deep breath as the tip poked a pinprick hole in my skin.

The knife moved away. I heard the sound of a cap being removed from a bottle, and then my nostrils burned as a chloroform-soaked rag was shoved against my face. Everything went blurry, and I returned to the wonderful world of unconsciousness.

* * *

I woke up in a ditch. There are much worse places to wake up, such as tied to a chair with a burlap sack over your head in a room with a brutal killer, but it's still not the most delightful waking experience. I was lying on my side in the mud, with a nice sharp stick poking me in the thigh.

To my great surprise, Roger was there as well. I could barely see him in the dark, but he was lying on his back with his eyes closed.

I sat up, letting out a small groan as my brain neglected to rise with the rest of my body. I reached over and prodded Roger's ankle. "Roger...?"

He moaned something that was probably "Huh?"

"You alive?"

"I don't know yet. I doubt it."

I pulled up my sleeve, but the face of my light-up wristwatch had been shattered so I couldn't tell what time it was. Since it was still dark, Helen wouldn't be off work and wouldn't have the entire police force looking for me yet.

"Do you think you can walk?" I asked.

"Ask me in a few minutes," he said, though I could barely hear him. "I'm still working on whether or not I'm alive."

I got to a standing position, nearly losing my balance as my legs tried to give way beneath me, then stepped over to where Roger lay. I reached down and offered my hand. "Come on, we need to get out of here."

I pulled him to his feet. The arrow had been removed and his leg had been tightly wrapped with a cloth. "There's no way I can walk on my own," he said. "But I know how much you like it when I lean against you, so if you'll be a pal and keep me steady I can probably come with you to civilization." He glanced around the area. "Wherever the hell that may be."

"Nowhere around here, that's for sure," I said. "How's your back?"

"Hurts. But there's something wrapped under my shirt, so I think the bleeding's been taken care of. If I start gushing I'll be sure to let you know."

We got ourselves out of the ditch and began to walk along the side of the road, with Roger holding onto my shoulder for balance. I guess it would have been more dramatic had I been able to carry him rather than merely assist him in limping along, but unfortunately my best friend wasn't a tiny woman.

And why was he here at all? Why the whole setup about not calling the police if Roger was just going to be dumped in the ditch along with me?

"I miss anything important?" asked Roger, as we walked along the lonely, deserted road.

"Yeah. Jennifer was stabbed to death."

"Jesus. You saw it?"

"I heard it." I filled him in on everything that had happened since I'd been bashed with the chain. Roger shook his head with disbelief.

"So I came really close to never waking up again," he said with a shiver. "It's been a really good night to be a hypocrite and turn to religion."

"Well, I figure there are two explanations for you being released with me. Either something went really wrong, and the killer couldn't afford to keep you around, or he already got whatever he was looking for and didn't need you any more."

"Or else he has something worse in store," said Roger. "Who would have thought that the simple act of digging up a grave could get so complicated? And we didn't even get the twenty thousand bucks."

About fifteen minutes later, headlights washed over us as a beat-up pickup truck drove around a corner. I stuck out my thumb and it came to a stop beside us. The driver leaned over, threw open the passenger door, and gave us a look of surprise.

"Gosh, you're exactly the kind of people my mom would've told me never to pick up!"

The driver was a heavyset guy with glasses and a thick gray beard. He wore a bright red baseball cap with "Kiss Me" written on it. He was in his sixties or seventies...it was hard to say for sure, because his face sort of looked like somebody had yanked his skull out through his mouth then shoved it back in slightly crooked.

"Well, my mother always said never to hitchhike, so I guess we're even," I said.

"Hop on in, you two," said the driver, patting the seat next to him. "Actually, lemme find a towel to put on the seat first. No offense, of course."

"None taken."

He fished around on the floor until he found a towel that didn't look much cleaner than we were and spread it out on the seat. I helped Roger in, and then sat down next to him, shutting the door behind me.

"Where're you headed?" the driver asked.

"To the nearest phone."

The truck began to move again. "What can I call you two?"

I pointed to Roger. "This is Roger Tanglen, and I'm Andrew Mayhem."

"Mayhem? That's an interestin' last name."

"Yeah, I think it explains a lot about my life. So what do we call you?"

"You can just call me The Apparition."

Roger and I exchanged a resigned look. With the kind of night we'd been having I guess it made perfect sense that we'd be picked up by a weirdo. "Any special reason?"

"Nope. Just like the way it sounds. You two are lookin' a little bit injured, if you don't mind my sayin' so. What happened?"

"A rampaging weed whacker got us. We fought hard but in the end we were just no match for it."

"That's about what it looks like. I think there might be a rag or something in the glove compartment if you wanna clean up a bit."

I thanked him and found the rag. It appeared to have

been used to clean heavy machinery, but I didn't want to be rude. I dusted my face off a bit, and then handed it to Roger.

"Looks like you took a few good hits," the Apparition noted, looking at me.

"Well, some of these marks are from last week's beating, not tonight's," I explained.

I began to straighten out my rumpled clothes. As I brushed off my leg, I noticed that something was stuck to the mud on my jeans. I pulled it off and held it up to examine it.

"What's that?" asked Roger.

"I'm not sure. Can I turn on the overhead light?"

"Be my guest," said The Apparition.

I flipped on the overhead light and saw that it appeared to be the corner of a playing card, though not from a traditional deck. It had the number 1 and depicted what looked like the end of a forked tail.

"I don't know what this is," I admitted. "Maybe it's Satanist currency. A Devil Dollar."

"I hate those damn Satanists," The Apparition muttered. "I haven't met any, but I sure have read about 'em, and what I've read I hate."

I put the corner of the card in my pocket. It probably wasn't important, but it also wasn't exactly going to weigh me down. And any clue might be helpful if I wanted to track down the killer, not that I was necessarily going to try and do so.

"Do you know what time it is?" I asked.

"The radio said it was about two-thirty, but I forget how long ago that was."

"Thanks," I said. I shared another look with Roger, and we made a silent pact to keep speech to a minimum for the rest of the ride.

* * *

The Apparition dropped us off at a convenience store and wished us luck in our future endeavors, especially if they involved bringing harm to Satanists. After finding out from the clerk that it was almost four and that we were thirty miles from Chamber, I went to the pay phone and dug out a quarter. I also thought to check for my wallet, and was pleasantly surprised to find that it hadn't been stolen.

"Andrew?" asked Helen, after one of her co-workers finally retrieved her. "Are you okay?"

"Um, no, not really. I'm here with Roger. Do you think you could get off early?"

"I'll have to do some pleading, but yeah, if it's an emergency of course I can. What happened?"

"I'll explain it all when I see you. By the way, could you be a sweetheart and bring stuff to help tend to a couple of arrow wounds?"

After giving the specifics on my location, I hung up and we went inside to buy a few Hershey's bars. The talk with my wife was not going to be pretty, and we were going to need a serious sugar buzz to get through it.

CHAPTER FIVE

When Helen finally made it to the convenience store, I gave her one of the candy bars as a peace offering, though I was pretty certain that the astounding power of chocolate wasn't going to get me out of this one. She reacted to our injuries with no small degree of concern, and insisted on checking out Roger's wounds right there in the parking lot.

"What on earth happened to you guys?" she demanded.

"Maybe you should wait until you're done fixing him before I explain," I said. "I'd really hate for you to make a mistake because you were pissed."

She regarded me intently, and then agreed that might be a good idea and took off Roger's shirt. "Whoever did this certainly wasn't a doctor," she said, unwrapping the cloth. "Can you lift your arms above your head?"

Roger did so with a wince.

"It got you in the shoulder blade. A couple inches to the right and you could've been paralyzed for life. That's why you shouldn't hang around my husband."

She cleaned out the wound and redressed it, assuring Roger that he was going to be okay. The leg wound was also not going to cause permanent damage, though Roger would definitely be on crutches for a while.

"And I'm driving you two to the hospital for x-rays, just in case," she said. "Don't argue."

I'm pretty stupid on a regular basis, but I wasn't stupid enough to argue.

As Helen drove us back to Chamber, Roger in the back seat, me in the hot seat, I told her the truth about what had happened. Okay, that's a lie. If I'd told her what really happened, she would have been an absolute nervous wreck and I would have been dead from the stress of living with a woman in that state of anxiety.

I wanted to stick to the truth as much as possible, unappealing as it was, so I confessed about the graverobbing bit. However, in the censored version, we'd been caught by a couple of hunters before we could unearth the coffin. Things got seriously out of hand, things were said, arrows were fired, and we ended up getting the crap beat out of us.

The story sounded credible as I told it, but to be honest my thought patterns were so shaky by this time that I could have been telling my wife that a magical turnip had inflicted our injuries and it would have sounded logical. To Helen's credit, she allowed me to finish my story before freaking out.

"What in God's name were you *thinking*?" she demanded. "What kind of sick, twisted, demented, deviant thoughts were running through your minds to make you agree to do that? I absolutely cannot believe that the man I married, the father of my children, would do something so appalling!"

"I had no idea it was going to turn out this way," I said. "I thought we'd dig a hole, grab a key, and go home twenty thousand dollars richer. Nice simple evening."

"This is just...I mean...it's just...I mean...holy shit, Andrew!"

"I agree."

Helen took several deep breaths. "Okay, look, I am so mad at you right now that I can't possibly verbalize it without an aneurysm, but we're not going to get into that right now. You've had an incredibly traumatic experience and I don't want to make things worse for you. But once you're healed, things are going to be very bad for you."

* * *

The hospital visit revealed that I did not have a concussion and that if I wanted my face to continue to look nice I was going to have to quit letting people punch me. It also confirmed that Roger's leg and back were going to heal fine, and that he was totally incompetent at walking on crutches. Fortunately, Helen agreed not to call the police to investigate the abusive hunters, since we'd have to explain why Roger and I were in the woods.

Instead of dropping Roger off at home, we decided to have him sleep at our place. While Helen took a shower, I opened the foldout bed on the couch and spoke quietly with him.

"We obviously can't go the police," I said, "but we've got to investigate, see what we can find out."

"Why?"

"Because the killer's still out there!"

"Yeah, but he got what he wanted, there's no reason for him to come after us," Roger insisted.

"You're right, but, I dunno, there's some weird instinct inside me saying that somebody who buries a man alive and stabs a woman to death shouldn't be allowed to get away with it. What do you think?"

"My leg hurts."

"Look, you don't have to help if you don't want to, but I'm going to try and find out what the whole deal is. So what do we know? Our suspect is acquainted with either Jennifer or Michael Ashcraft or both. Probably both. Vicious right hook. Decent archer. What am I missing?"

Roger had nothing to add.

"Okay, so it's not much, but it's a start." I took the business card out of my pocket. "First thing tomorrow, I'll find out what this Ghoulish Delights thing is. Maybe we'll get lucky and the killer will be hanging around in bloodstained clothes."

Roger shrugged. "Could I have an extra pillow?"

Helen's shower ended. As I heard the hair dryer turn on, I quickly looked through the phone book and found Michael Ashcraft's name. I dialed the number and got his answering machine. It was a man's voice, presumably Michael's. He sounded a little different when he wasn't shrieking.

"Hi, you've reached the residence of Michael and Jennifer Ashcraft. We're going to be on vacation until the first of September, but if you leave your name and number at the tone we'll get back to you when we return. By the way, we have a state of the art security system and a couple of really vicious Dobermans named Rabid Assassin I and Rabid Assassin II, so any potential thieves may want to find a safer target, such as Fort Knox. Ready yourself, here comes the beep."

So nobody was likely to be looking for them. I hung up.

I sat on my bed and stared at the wall for a few minutes until Helen came out of the bathroom. "Honey, you aren't even undressed. You really should get some sleep."

"Well, I got a little bit of sleep after I was knocked unconscious."

Helen sighed. "Don't make jokes."

I took off my clothes and got into bed, even though in my spooked condition I figured there was no way I'd be able to fall asleep without an elephant tranquilizer.

As it turns out, I was wrong. I managed about three hours of sleep, though with the worst nightmares I'd had in my entire life. And I'm counting the recurring dream of Mr. Boogedy-Bones from pre-school.

* * *

After I got out of bed and showered the nightmare sweat from my body, I dressed in jeans and a t-shirt. I called the number on the Ghoulish Delights card and got another answering machine.

"Thank you for calling Ghoulish Delights, where we make your worst fears a reality," said Michael's voice. "Our office hours are by appointment only, but if you leave your name and number at the tone we'll get back to you as soon as possible."

I hung up, figuring I'd try back later.

So, what next? I had Michael's street address from the phone book, so I'd pay a visit to his house to see if there was anything of interest. After that, I supposed that I could find out the names of Jennifer and Michael's friends and family and just start going down the list, but what would I say? "Hi, I'm doing a survey on premature burial habits in the Chamber area. Have you or anyone you know buried a person alive within the past week?" I couldn't ask "Where were you on the night of August fourth, between midnight and 4 a.m.?" because anyone could say "I was in bed sleeping, you brain-dead moron!" and it would be almost impossible to prove them wrong.

I left Roger asleep on the couch and set a note on the nightstand for Helen that read "Went out." At least that kept me entirely truthful.

As I was on my way to Halloway Street, where Michael lived, I came up on the Chamber Eastside Mall. Remembering that they had a game store inside, I decided to make a quick detour and see if the piece of card I'd found last night could be identified.

I pulled into the parking lot, went inside, turned down a free sample of nasty-looking Bourbon chicken from a vendor in the food court, and proceeded to Gamer's Castle.

"Hi," said the gawky teenager behind the counter. I nodded and briefly looked through the racks of role-playing game merchandise. There was Dungeons and Dragons stuff out the wazoo, and even kits for hosting your own murder mystery parties, should I ever grow weary of having my murder mystery needs satisfied by real life.

"Are you looking for anything in particular?" the teenager asked.

"Actually, yes," I said, approaching the counter and taking out the piece of card. "Could you tell me which game this belongs to?"

He took the card from me, glanced at it for a split second, the handed it back. "Oh, sure, it's a level one imp. It's one of the weakest characters in Prophecies of the Night. They're very common, not collectible at all."

"Prophecies of the Night? I've never heard of it."

"That's not surprising. It's really not very popular. It has a very weak character generation system, not anywhere near as realistic as the designer's last couple of games. But he was having personal problems and a tight deadline on this one, so it's understandable."

"Of course," I agreed.

"We returned a bunch of stuff to the distributor, but we have a few enemy decks left if you're interested. That's where the piece you've got came from."

"Well, if it has an unrealistic character generation system I'll probably have to pass. You wouldn't happen to know of any groups that play regularly, would you?"

The teenager shook his head. "Nah. Like I said, it's not very popular. Actually, you could check the bulletin board against the far wall in case somebody posted one and I didn't notice, but I'm pretty sure there's not."

I walked back to the bulletin board, which was covered with index cards advertising gaming groups. I took a few moments to scan them, but the teenager had been right, there were none for Prophecies of the Night. Oh well. It was a long shot anyway.

I was about to thank the teenager and leave, but something stopped me. Okay, all I'd found was a tiny little piece of card stuck to my jeans. But unless it was already in the ditch, it had to have got there when the killer was moving me, and so there was a good chance that he was a player. And I'd read a few mystery novels, enough to know that it was usually the insignificant clue that solved the case.

I returned to the counter. "Actually, I'd like a deck of those cards, if you don't mind."

"No problem." The teenager left the counter and returned an instant later holding a small deck. He punched some keys on the cash register. "That'll be eighteen eighty."

"Say what?"

"Eighteen dollars and eighty cents, including tax."

"For a deck of cards?"

"Yeah."

"No, no, no, cards don't cost eighteen dollars and eighty cents," I explained. "Cards cost a buck or two. A little more if they have naked women on them."

"You're not a seasoned gamer, are you?"

"Obviously not."

"I can give you a ten percent discount if you join our Gamer's Castle frequent buyer club. It costs ten dollars and is good for a full year."

"No, thanks, I'll pay retail." I dug out my wallet and grudgingly handed him a twenty, hoping that these damn cards at least came with bubble gum. "By the way, you wouldn't happen to know a Michael Ashcraft, would you?"

The teenager thought for a moment. "Nope."

"Jennifer Ashcraft?"

"Nope."

"Okay. Thanks for your help."

* * *

Not being Sherlock Holmes has its disadvantages. While Sherlock would have been able to solve the whole mystery based on the composition of the dirt on the jeans I wore last night, I managed to pretty much bumble around for the next couple hours without learning anything of interest. I stopped at Michael's house, a fairly nice one-story deal in the suburbs, but the neighbors on one side were having a yard sale, and the neighbor on the other side was out mowing his lawn, so I decided it would be best to postpone any serious investigating.

I returned home to find that my mother-in-law had just brought the kids back, so we sat down to a soup and sandwich lunch. I tried to be a cheerful daddy, but with everything that was on my mind it was difficult to be as immature as my kids would have liked, even while listening to Kyle's vivid description of yesterday's activities.

"An' we played Squish the Bug an' we—"

"It's Stomp the Bug, stupid," Theresa corrected in that special way big sisters have.

"An' we played Stomp the Bug an' Theresa was the bug six times an' I was only the bug four times an' then Aunt Marcia came an' she took us to get frozen yogurt an' I got chocolate vanilla swirl an' Theresa got regular chocolate an' she dropped her cone in Aunt Marcia's car an' Aunt Marcia got mad an' said not to drop her cone again or she wouldn't be allowed to have food in the car an' Theresa said okay."

"Wow, busy night," I said.

"Yeah. An' we watched *The Elrod McBugle Show*. Elrod drank a whole swimming pool an' everyone who was swimming got mad."

"Will you take us swimming, Daddy?" asked Theresa.

"I can't today, sweetie. Daddy has stuff to do. But I promise I'll take you pretty soon. Just play outside today, but remember what I said about staying away from the boy next door. Anyone who tries to feed you kitty litter is not a true friend."

"Are you going off to be a freeloader?" Kyle inquired.

Helen nearly choked on a spoonful of soup. "Where did you hear that?" she asked.

"Aunt Marcia. What does 'freeloader' mean?"

I decided to field that one. "It means your Aunt Marcia

needs to keep her enormous mouth—"

Helen cut me off. "It means Daddy is currently testing various career opportunities."

"Oh," said Kyle, nodding with understanding.

Roger grinned. "Testing various career opportunities. That's exactly the way I would have phrased it."

"Shut up," I said.

"Daddy, you're not supposed to tell people to shut up," Theresa informed me.

"Roger doesn't count. You can tell him to shut up all you want."

"Shut up, shut up, shut up," sang Kyle.

"Andrew, please don't talk to our children any more than is absolutely necessary," said Helen.

Around one, I called again.

"Hello, Ghoulish Delights, where we make your nightmares a reality. Rachel speaking. How may I help you?"

"Hi," I said. "I'm calling for Michael Ashcraft."

"Oh, I'm sorry. He's out of town. Is this something I can help you with?"

"Possibly. I was given one of your business cards, and I have to admit that the name sounds very intriguing. What exactly do you do there?"

"Do you like horror movies?"

"Love 'em."

"Then you'll probably like what we do. You know, if you want to stop on by, we'd be more than happy to give you a tour."

"Sure, why not?" I said. "I've got some spare time. When should I be there?"

"We should be hanging around until about five, so any time before that. Do you need directions?"

"Nope. I'll see you soon, then. Thanks!"

After putting on a new watch and assuring Helen about sixty-eight times that we were both feeling fine and that it wasn't necessary for us to stay at home to recuperate, Roger and I drove to the address on the card. Ghoulish Delights looked like somebody's house that had been converted into a business, bearing only a small sign in the same oozing letters as on the card.

After narrowly avoiding a serious crutch mishap, we stepped onto the porch and rang the doorbell. It was answered by a tall, athletically-built, dark-haired woman who wore a t-shirt with the Ghoulish Delights logo.

"Hi, I'm Rachel Mallory," she said, extending her hand. I noticed that she wore black fingernail polish, with a little eyeball drawn on each nail. It was pretty cool.

"Andrew Mayhem. This is my friend Roger."

"Pleased to meet you. Welcome to our lair."

We walked inside. The waiting room had a couch, a couple of chairs, a small table, and a wall that had every square inch covered with horror movie posters. One of the chairs was currently occupied by a skeleton wearing a pair of bunny ears and smoking a cigarette.

"That's our mascot, Calcium," said Rachel. "Have a seat on the couch and I'll introduce the others to you." She went over and poked her head into the adjoining room. "Potential customers are here! Everyone act your weirdest!"

Four other people marched out of the room. "Why don't you all introduce yourselves and tell these nice men what it is you do around here," said Rachel.

The first guy looked about thirty, wore thick glasses, had short blonde hair with a huge cowlick, and a very ruddy complexion with several streaks of acne. "I'm Carl Underall," he said, looking to the left of me instead of making eye contact. "Cameraman."

Next to him was a small, thin, red-headed, freckle-faced guy in his mid-twenties. He wore a Ghoulish Delights t-shirt like Rachel's, except that this one had a fake hand protruding from the stomach holding...well, a stomach. "I'm Farley Soukup," he said in a squeaky voice that immediately forced me to hate him. "Special effects."

The next guy was also in his mid-twenties. He had a dark complexion and was dressed entirely in black. His straight black hair hung over his shoulders, and he even wore black nail polish and a black dangling spider earring—a Goth boy through and through. It wouldn't have surprised me if he'd been wearing a set of vampire teeth. If I'd been holding a glass, the temptation to fling the contents at him and scream

"Holy water!" would have been unbearable. "Dominick Griffin," he said. "Sound, story and occasional on-camera predator."

"And I'm Linda Hanson," said the girl next to him, who was obviously his girlfriend, judging from the arm coiled around his waist. She was also dressed entirely in black, but she added bleach-blonde hair and blood-red lipstick to the color palette. She was a little overweight, but her tight-fitting clothing indicated that she was comfortable with her body. She flashed me a cheerful smile. "Set decoration, lighting, and props. Welcome to our happy home."

"Thanks," I said. "So this is a movie studio, huh? Would I have seen any of your films?"

Rachel gave the others a wave to indicate that they could go back to their business, and then sat down on one of the chairs. "So, Michael gave you a card but didn't say anything about what we do here?"

"Actually, it was at a party a while back. I'd had a lot to drink and I don't really remember the conversation, but the name, Ghoulish Delights, sounded pretty intriguing. I've kept meaning to call, but this is the first day off I've had in a while. Some people call me a workaholic."

"Well, hopefully you'll think we're as cool as our name. You say you're a horror movie fan?"

"Sure," I said. "I love all that stuff. The movies, the books, the games, everything. Guess I'm just a sicko at heart."

"I can handle them if the characters aren't too stupid," Roger said.

"Let me ask you this," said Rachel. "Have you ever wanted to star in your very own horror flick?"

"Some days I feel like I already am," I told her.

Rachel leaned forward. "What we do here at Ghoulish Delights is create a short, custom-made horror film for you and your family and friends to star in, which we can tape in your very own home or anywhere else you want. We have a large selection of script templates, which are completely customizable to suit whatever strikes your fancy. If you'd like your family of four to star in their very own mad-slasher-in-the-house flick, we can give you the script, the stage directions, and all the blood and gore you could ever want. You're both too old to belong to a fraternity...no offense...but last week we pretended to kill off sixteen guys in their very own frat house. It's fun!"

"Do you get a lot of business for this sort of thing?" I asked.

Rachel shrugged. "We're doing all right. Our office is located here in Chamber, but very few of our customers come from this area. We head out all over Florida, to Miami, Tampa...and some occasional tourist business in Orlando, for people who want something a little darker than Disney World."

"So you just come to somebody's house and shoot it like a regular movie?"

"Pretty much. You could think of it as a slightly more offbeat version of family portraits. How it works is you would describe the locale you want and the number of actors you have, and then we'd show you our sample scripts. After you found one you liked, we'd revise it to make it a perfect match for your group, and then assign the roles. Don't worry, everyone gets a good part. We'd come over, and our director would work with your people while our guys set everything up, then we'd film until we got it right. It usually takes most of the day, and everyone has a great time. And when we're done you have a ten to fifteen minute video that's yours to keep."

"And there aren't any limits? You get to do whatever you want?"

"Oh, no, obviously we have both safety precautions and technology restraints. We're not going to film your three year-old daughter hanging out of a second floor window, and the only explosives we can get the insurance for are tiny squibs to simulate a gunshot wound."

"Squibs?" asked Roger.

"It's a balloon that's filled with stage blood and hooked up to a small explosive charge. When you set it off, blood sprays and it looks like you were shot. Some effects artists use a condom instead of a balloon, but since we often have kids around we try not to do anything that adds to their sexual confusion."

"That's very thoughtful," I said.

"And we do strictly below-the-neck squibs. So we do have a few restrictions that are simply for safety reasons, because a horror movie stops being fun when people really get hurt.

And, like I said, there are things we simply can't do. We have people saying 'Why can't you show me transforming into a werewolf?' and it's because we don't have the resources. We do have a large supply of monster masks and costumes, and can do minor monster makeup, but you're not going to get state-of-the-art special effects—it's not feasible for what we're trying to do here. We can't show your son's head rolling down the stairs, because that involves making a cast, but we can certainly use camera tricks and makeup to simulate a decapitation. And Karo syrup is cheap, so you can have all the blood you want. So, have I frightened you off yet?"

Actually, I thought it was a pretty neat idea. But then, I guess I've always been kind of strange. There'd been many times over the past few years when I'd been able to easily envision Kyle or Theresa turning into mass murderers, and it would probably be fun to see this captured on video. Yet somehow I just couldn't see Helen finding the idea to her liking. And it was probably expensive as hell.

Anyway, I wasn't here as a customer, I was here to gather information. "Okay, time to fess up," I said. "I didn't get your card from a party. I'm really a journalist. Have you heard of the magazine *Dearly Demented*?"

Rachel shook her head. This was good, because I'd made up the magazine and would have hated to be quizzed on the contents had it turned out to be a real one.

"That's not surprising, since our premiere issue is still four months away. Our target audience is comprised of those people who are interested in the darker side of life, but in a fun way, of course. And I think a feature article on Ghoulish Delights would fit exactly with what my editor is looking for."

"Really? Who's your editor?"

I gestured to Roger. "Him. He doesn't quite trust me out on my own yet."

It would have been more believable to say Roger was my photographer, but that kind of lie generally works better when one is in possession of a camera.

"We've actually had a few stories done on us," Rachel remarked. "Mostly just local newspapers, though channel eight sent a camera crew out last Halloween and did a short feature. It was sort of slanted toward calling us a bunch of sick lunatics, but we got a couple of gigs out of it."

"Well, I can assure you that if *Dearly Demented* called you a bunch of sick freaks, it would be a wholehearted compliment."

Rachel smiled. "We'd be honored to have you do a story on our little outfit. Would you like a tour now, or would you like to set another appointment?"

"What would work best for me is if I could just talk to each person, find out exactly what it is they do for Ghoulish Delights. For example, what exactly do you do?"

"At the moment I'm doing my job and Michael's...that's Michael Ashcraft, our director...so I'd be absolutely overwhelmed if business weren't slow right now. Basically, I'm the producer, so I'm responsible for overseeing, well, everything. I do most of the interaction with the customer, from the interesting and informative sales pitch you just heard to making sure they're happy with the condition of their home afterward. And I'm responsible for all the financial aspects of the business, making sure we run things as cheaply as possible so we don't price ourselves out of reach."

"What does something like this cost?" Roger asked.

"The price varies substantially based on what options the customer requests, sort of like a new car."

"How much for a base model?"

Rachel smiled again. "To be completely honest, we prefer to wait until a customer is completely enraptured before springing the cost on the poor person."

"That bad, huh?"

"Well...it's more expensive than taking the family out to play miniature golf."

I nodded my understanding. It suddenly occurred to me that this whole reporter charade would work better if I actually had a small notebook or a tape recorder. I considered making a comment like "So, Roger, is the ol' photographic memory storing everything all right?" but that would have been stupid. I probably should have planned a cover story before driving over here. The idea that I really suck as a detective crossed my mind.

"So was this whole thing your idea?" I asked.

"No, it was Mike's. We were friends all through college, and we'd rent maybe six or seven horror movies every weekend. We'd just sit in his dorm room and toxify our brains watching these things. We sort of went our separate ways after he graduated, partially because his girlfriend, now his wife, was jealous of all the time we spent together...not that you need to write anything about that." She suddenly looked worried. "You're not going to use that quote, are you?"

"Not if you don't want me to," I assured her.

"Oh, good. It sort of slipped out. Anyway, I stayed in Chamber and was working full time as a trainer at the gym, and Mike moved from place to place trying and failing to carve out a career as a filmmaker. We met up again two years ago just by coincidence. Some friends came from out of town and wanted to do the theme park thing, so I took them to Universal Studios, and there Mike was, working as a photographer at the King Kong ride. We met up later that night and he told me about this whole idea for making custom-made horror movies. Oh, by the way, can I get you some coffee?"

"No, I'm fine," I said.

"I just now thought of that. I'd hate you to start your article with 'Ghoulish Delights is run by Rachel Mallory, a woman who likes to talk and talk and talk and talk without so much as having the courtesy to provide refreshments.'"

"No, really, I'm okay. Roger's fine too. Please continue."

"Basically, I thought it sounded like a lot of fun, though I wasn't sure if it was something we could actually make money at. Well, we couldn't get a bank loan to save our lives, so finally Mike swallowed his pride, called up his rich brother, and begged for the start-up money. He got it, we rented this place, and then he started calling people he knew wouldn't demand a regular paycheck. Pretty soon we had Carl, Farley, Linda, and Dominick, and we were set."

"And you're all making a living at this now?"

"Not a great one, but we do okay. To be completely honest, we don't make all of our money from Ghoulish Delights. We have to film the occasional wedding or bar mitzva, but overall we're not starving to death."

"What does Mike's wife think of Ghoulish Delights?"

Rachel shrugged. "I don't see her much. Every once in a while she'll come in here and turn up her nose at one of Farley's creatures, but that's about it."

"But she'd rather he take some steady-paying job, right?"

"Of course. I'm sure she makes more with her waitress

job than he does here. But then, she's sort of a—" Rachel held her hands out in front of her chest, miming substantial breasts, "—impressive woman, so good tips probably aren't hard to come by."

I began to feel a bit uncomfortable. Rachel certainly felt no love for Jennifer Ashcraft. She didn't seem anything like the murderous type, but then again, John Wayne Gacy performed at children's parties as Pogo the Clown, yet still murdered thirty-three people. Of course, clowns can be pretty scary.

Michael could have been having an affair with Rachel, and it could have turned ugly. I wasn't sure what kind of ugly end to an affair might result in Michael being buried alive holding a revolver, but it was possible. Yet if Rachel was the killer, would she be sitting here confessing that she didn't like Jennifer? And she'd been genuinely friendly, not giving any indication that she might have tied me up last night and pressed a bloody knife against my neck.

No, it couldn't be Rachel.

Probably.

"Is it all right if I talk to the others now?" I asked.

"No problem. Let's go on back."

CHAPTER SEVEN

The main part of the house was a large room, maybe forty by sixty feet, that was simply jam-packed with neat stuff. One wall was entirely overtaken by a rack of costumes. Above the rack was a shelf upon which rested a long line of Halloween masks, everything from Frankenstein to an undead boy scout to Richard Simmons. Another wall display contained dozens of (I assume) fake weapons: axes, knives, spears, chainsaws, etc. The room was also loaded with camera equipment, videotapes, buckets of paint, blueprints, storyboard paintings, and one large table in the center. There was also a small doorway, minus an actual door, which led somewhere unknown. Carl, Dominick, and Linda were all huddled around the table, playing with *Star Wars* action figures, while Farley added some white paint to a piece of rubber.

Among the weapons, I noticed a crossbow.

"So, do we have another customer?" asked Farley, looking up as we entered.

"Actually, these gentlemen are from *Dearly Demented* magazine, here to do a story on us," Rachel told him. "Be nice to them."

"Never heard of that one," said Farley.

"Premiere issue is four months away," I explained. "But it's going to be flashy, don't worry."

Farley gestured toward Roger's crutches. "The magazine

business is dangerous, huh?"

"More dangerous than you can imagine," said Roger. "Those computer terminals can be deadly. Hurt my leg typing an adjective. Happens all the time."

"Anyway," said Rachel, "I want each of you to talk to the nice men, tell them what you do around here."

"Right now we're having a great battle between Chewbacca and a couple of Stormtroopers," said Linda. "This is what we get paid for. Life is good."

"Actually, they're blocking out a new plot scenario," Rachel told us. "Normally I'd be working with them, but I was busy sucking up to you two. Hey, Farley, why don't you show them what you're doing?"

We walked over to where Farley stood. There were several identical pieces of rubber spread out on the table in front of him. He finished adding a bit of white paint to the one he was working on, then set it down to dry. "What I'm doing right now is making generic wounds out of latex. These are throat wounds, as you can clearly see from the protruding windpipe." He tapped the protruding windpipe with his index finger to make sure we clearly saw it. "I've got all different kinds of wounds and scars, and when they're needed I just apply them to the actor with rubber cement, use makeup to make sure it blends with the skin, and then add a big dollop of blood. Instant carnage. Fun for all ages."

"Do you make these yourself?" I asked.

"Absolutely. There're a lot of places you can order them from, but what fun is that?" Farley gave me a wicked grin. "How would you like a torn-out throat?"

"Nah, I make it a point never to simulate throat rippings this early in the day, but maybe next time," I said.

"Oh, come on," said Farley, picking up one of the fake wounds. "If you really wanna understand the inner workings of Ghoulish Delights, you've gotta get a little dirty. Dominick, you wanna slide a chair over here and grab a sheet?"

"No, seriously, that's okay. I'm allergic to latex. That's why I have two kids. However, I'm sure Roger would love to have part of his neck removed, wouldn't you, Roger?"

"Huh?"

Dominick pushed a chair over to where we stood. "Have a seat, Roger," said Farley. "We'll get you messed up real good."

Roger started to protest, but instead settled for giving me a dirty look as he sat down in the chair. The others stopped playing with their action figures and watched with amusement. Dominick handed Farley a small white sheet, which he draped over Roger's chest like a bib.

"Be gentle with me, I'm crippled," said Roger.

"You'll be more than crippled when I'm done with you," Farley informed him. He began to apply a generous portion of rubber cement to the latex. "Tilt your head back. Further. Further. Good."

He carefully positioned the latex in the center of Roger's neck, and then pressed down on it firmly. I had another uncomfortable moment as I realized that with one violent push Farley could probably crush Roger's throat. I was getting seriously paranoid.

"Now you have to sit here perfectly still while it dries," Farley said.

"Oh, joy," Roger muttered.

"Don't talk, either. Okay, Andrew, you can move on to your next tour station. I'll call you back when we're ready."

I figured leaving Roger there unable to move as sticky stuff dried on his neck was suitable punishment for one of the many pranks he'd played on me over the years, so I walked over to Carl. "You're the cameraman, right?"

"That's right." Carl shrugged. "Not sure exactly what I should tell you. I point the camera where stuff is happening and try to keep it in focus, basically."

"Could I see your equipment?"

"Yeah, if you want." Carl led me to the other side of the room, where the camera equipment was stored. I had no real interest in seeing it, but I wanted to speak with Carl away from the others.

"So how did you get into Ghoulish Delights?"

"Mike Ashcraft asked me. He and Rachel were the ones who started this. He's our director but he's on vacation." Carl alternated between looking at me and the floor when he talked.

"Yeah, Rachel told me. So, were you two friends, or classmates, or did you work together on another project, or...?"

"Worked at the Legacy Six theatre together. Used to fight over who got to keep the good movie posters."

"So what's he like? I mean, what kind of person comes

up with an idea like Ghoulish Delights?"

Another shrug. "He's a little askew, like the rest of us. Nice guy. Doesn't try to tell me what to do when I'm taping, so he's pretty easy to work with." He thought for a long moment. "Aside from that, I don't know what else to say."

I asked him about the cameras, just so he'd think I was interested. He spouted off some technical specifications that meant absolutely nothing to me, but I nodded as he spoke. When he'd finished, I thanked him and turned back to the throat ripping demonstration. "Is he ready yet?"

"Not yet," said Farley. "The actors always hate this part. I know I do. That's why I stay on this side of the special effects."

Roger didn't look like he was enjoying this much, which was all right. I walked back over to the action figure setup. "What exactly does this represent?" I asked Linda.

"This is just a scenario we're working on," she replied. "We have about twenty of them right now, but we try to add more whenever we've got some downtime. The more variety we have, the easier it is to find something that appeals to the customers."

"What kinds of scenarios do you have in your collection right now?"

"For the most part, they're just variations on the stalk-and-slash theme. We're not making movies for commercial release, so we don't need shocking plot twists or bold new concepts. Essentially a Ghoulish Delights movie involves somebody running around killing everyone else." She explained this in a remarkably perky voice, as if she were hosting a cooking show.

"Hey, that's all I need in a movie," I said.

"Most of the work is done after the customer has selected their scenario. Technically, one of the scripts could be filmed as-is—it has dialogue and everything. But since we never know where we're going to shoot it, and we can't possibly have a script already prepared for every possible combination of actors, we have to make a lot of small changes on the set. Plus, we're not dealing with professional actors here, so a lot of the time we'll have to tone down some of the dialogue or revise it to make it easier to deliver. Once we had a script comprised of nothing but screams and one line, 'Now you die!' And the guy ended up forgetting to say 'you.' Suffice it to say that we haven't started rehearsing our Academy Awards speech yet."

"Of course, my loving girlfriend here has just described *my* job," said Dominick good-naturedly. "I let her help sometimes, so she occasionally forgets that I'm the one in charge of the script."

"Actually, he doesn't *let* me help, I bully my way into it," said Linda.

"That's exactly right."

"But he loves a dominant woman."

"I don't remember asking for one at Christmas."

"That's because I wrote up your list for you, being a dominant woman."

"That figures."

"Oh, is my sweetie being sulky? Nobody likes being around a person with a stinky attitude, even if they have a cute little dent in their chin like you."

"If you keep it up, that Roger guy is going to want his throat torn out for real," Dominick told her.

I was getting to that point myself. I was also starting to notice that Dominick smelled kind of weird, but I couldn't identify the scent.

"I'm so sorry, sweetie, did I steal your glory by telling about what you do, with my help? Here, you can tell them what I do now."

"No, that's all right, I wouldn't want you to stop being the center of attention."

"Good." Linda turned back to me. "I do all the set decoration and prop work, except for weapons, which Dominick does."

"What kind of set decoration?" I asked. "Doesn't it take place in people's homes?"

"Usually their homes, or sometimes outdoors. I make sure furniture gets rearranged to fit what we need for the scene, and if the scene calls for somebody to be making cookies, I'll set that up, and stuff like that."

"Doesn't sound like she does much, does it?" asked Dominick. "That might explain why she feels the need to keep invading my territory."

She swatted him playfully on the arm. "I also do the lighting, which is very important in that it allows people to actually see themselves on the videotape."

"Essentially, her job is to go from room to room and find out where all the light switches are," Dominick said. "Once she's done that, she goes back and makes sure that they all operate on the up-for-on, down-for-off principal. Occasionally her job will be made more difficult with a knob instead of a switch, but that's what she makes the big bucks for."

She swatted him again, also playfully but with a hell of a lot more force than last time. "Actually, I work with very large, powerful lights, which I have to set up out of sight of the camera. And I have to make sure that they don't burn down the customer's home, which tends to screw up our chances of a good referral."

"I can see where that would prove problematic." I was still noticing Dominick's aroma, which I suspected was some kind of funky Goth cologne. "This is off the subject," I said, "but what kind of cologne are you wearing?"

Dominick frowned, then lifted his palm to his nose and sniffed. "Oh, that. Catfish."

"The mighty sportsman was out terminating helpless fish this morning," said Linda. "Those manly impulses get the best of him sometimes. Normally he does a better job bathing afterward."

Farley waved to me. "If you've had enough of the lover's quarrel, I think he's dry."

I returned to where poor Roger sat. "How's it going, buddy?" I asked. He gave me the finger on the sly, which I thought was shockingly unprofessional for a magazine editor.

Farley began to brush on some flesh-colored makeup, hiding the edge of the latex and making it look like a natural part of Roger's neck. "We do almost entirely aftermath gore here," he explained. "It's pretty complicated to actually *show* a throat being ripped out, and it definitely takes more time than we've got when we're just visiting somebody's house for a day. And it's a little more gruesome than most people want anyway, the wimps. So we won't actually show anything really gross happening, we'll just show what it looks like afterward."

He took a couple more minutes to blend in the makeup, and then nodded with satisfaction at the result. "Now, if this were for real, I'd take longer to ensure that it looks more believable, but this is just a demonstration. Dominick, could you grab me the bottle of blood?"

Dominick took a large bottle from one of the shelves and brought it to him. "Show of hands," said Farley. "Little bit of blood, or lot of blood? All in favor of little blood?"

Nobody but Roger raised their hands. I certainly didn't.

"Lot of blood?"

Everyone else raised their hands.

"Okay, let's dump it on!" Farley poured a generous portion of the blood on Roger's neck. It was thick and looked unnervingly real. "Enough? Never!" He poured on even more, and I could see Roger cringe as it oozed down the side of his neck.

"Am I dead yet?" he asked.

"Oh, yeah, you're dead," said Farley.

"Okay, roll your eyes in the back of your head and let your tongue hang out," said Rachel, appearing out of nowhere with a Polaroid camera. Roger did as instructed, and she snapped a picture. She removed the photo from the camera and handed it to me. "Here. This could be the cover of your magazine."

"Can I get up now?" asked Roger.

"If you want, I could add a small demonic creature gnawing on your throat," Farley offered. "I don't make this offer for everyone, so take it or forever hold your peace."

"I'll hold my peace," said Roger. Farley held the sheet so that it caught most of the blood as Roger sat up.

"Oops, it dripped a bit," Farley pointed out. "But that wasn't your best shirt anyway, was it?"

"Too bad Helen isn't working right now," I said. "We could pay a visit to the hospital and freak her out." After about .0037 of a second's reflection, I decided that it was, in fact, a *good* thing Helen wasn't working right now.

"I'll give you a free severed thumb effect if you walk around town all day wearing that and a sign that says 'Ghoulish Delights was here,'" Farley offered.

"Thanks, but no," said Roger. "How about directing me to the nearest bathroom?"

Linda took him by the hand. "Here, I'll show you." She led him through the doorway. After a moment's consideration,

Dominick followed.

"Could I look at one of the scripts?" I asked Rachel.

"Oh, sure, come on back to the waiting room," she said.

Looking at the script was just to satisfy my own curiosity. I really didn't have much to go on toward figuring out who buried Michael and stabbed Jennifer, but I was pretty sure it hadn't been anyone in Ghoulish Delights. After all, could I really stand there and talk to the killer face-to-face without getting any kind of indication that he or she hated my guts?

Rachel took a binder off her desk and handed it to me. I opened to the first script and quickly flipped through the ten pages. Linda was really on to something when she said they weren't practicing their Academy Awards speeches yet.

Sample dialogue:

MOTHER: Stay away! Stay away, you beast! Stay away!

PSYCHOPATH: Never! You will die, as did my own mother, and as will all the mothers of the world when I'm done!

MOTHER: But...but...it's Father's Day!

While I was perusing the script, Carl walked into the room and asked Rachel something very technical about a new tripod. She answered back with something equally technical and budget-related. Carl tried to explain in very technical terms why the budget-related answer wasn't what he wanted to hear, but Rachel quickly forced him to accept it, and he returned to the back room.

As I set the script back down, I noticed something resting on Rachel's desk that gave my heart a sudden jolt. A deck of cards. Prophecies of the Night.

"Oh, hey, Prophecies of the Night," I said, keeping my voice casual. "Do you play?"

Rachel rolled her eyes. "Oh, God, Carl is always trying to foist that stupid game on us. He plays it once a week with his friends. He got everyone a deck for Christmas, and we all get a new deck on our birthday. I went with him once just to shut him up, but the game makes no sense."

"It is a bit confusing," I agreed, to keep her from giving me a pop quiz on the rules. "Is Carl the only one who plays regularly?"

"No, actually, I think Farley goes with him quite a bit, and Dominick and Linda will go occasionally just to mooch free chips and soda. I remember Mike saying something about shoving a fireplace poker through Carl's left nostril if he didn't shut up about that stupid game, so I don't think he's a regular."

"Do you know where they play? I've been looking for a player's group for a while, but I've never been able to find one."

"They play in the basement of Balder's Dash on Thursdays. As far as I know they're on for tonight, though you might want to ask Carl to make sure."

What a happy coincidence! I'd looked seven-to-one odds in the face and come out victorious!

"I don't think I'll be able to make it tonight," I lied, "but I might mention it to him some other time. So here're a couple of questions. First, could we possibly tag along when you're filming one of these things? And, second, is there some time we could meet, just us, to talk outside of work?"

"I hope you're not asking me out," she said. "I'm flattered, but I can very clearly see that little ball and chain around your ring finger."

"No, no, it's strictly professional. You look pretty strong, but my wife has access to a drawer full of kitchen knives and knows where I sleep. No, it's that whole human interest deal...what do the people who work at Ghoulish Delights do in their spare time?"

Roger walked into the waiting room with Linda, his throat intact again. "He's all yours," Linda told me with a wide grin.

"Thanks," I said. "Looking snazzy, Rog."

"I agree. Your throat has never looked better," Rachel commented. To me, she said "How about we meet tomorrow at Von's Gym, 6 A.M.?"

"Um, I've heard rumors that such an hour of the morning exists, but so far it's unconfirmed."

"Great, six o'clock then. I assume you don't have a membership, so you'll need to tell the guy at the front desk that you're there to see me. And as for tagging along with us, we have an appointment tomorrow at noon, and if you show up here around eleven we'll be more than happy to have you."

We thanked her and left the house. "Why do you think she assumed I don't have a gym membership?" I asked Roger as I shut the door behind me.

"I guess she missed all those muscles bursting through your shirt," he replied. "A common problem, to be honest."

"Shut up."

"You asked, I told. Hey, what's that on your car?"

There was indeed something on the hood of my car, a bright red box, about one foot square, covered with yellow stars. When we reached the car and saw it up close, it was revealed to be a jack-in-the-box.

"Okay, so what the hell is this all about?" Roger asked.

It was a perfectly innocent-looking jack-in-the-box, but I wasn't sure we were going to like the answer.

CHAPTER EIGHT

"It's no big deal," I said, trying to sound casual. "Just a jack-in-the-box. Turn the crank, hear a catchy tune, see a clown pop up, squeal with delight."

"Uh-huh. So why is it sitting here on your car?"

"That I can't answer."

"You think the killer put it here, as a warning?"

"How should I know? I don't even think anyone in there *is* the killer! One of them, or all of them, probably just stuck it out here as a prank. We'll turn the handle and see a clown with an axe in his head or something."

"Or it could explode and kill us both," Roger pointed out.

"Now you're getting a little paranoid. Do you think the killer just happened to have a booby-trapped jack-in-the-box sitting around in case we showed up?"

"I don't know, but I certainly welcome you to turn the handle and see what happens. I'll be way the hell over there behind that tree."

"Okay, look, this is stupid. I'll pick it up, march right back in there, and demand to know who put it out here."

"It could have been any of them," said Roger. "Rachel could've done it while I was in the back being tortured, and anyone else could've done it while we were in the waiting room."

"If there's a back door, yeah. Farley could have snuck out unnoticed when Carl came out to gripe about his tripod.

Were Dominick and Linda with you the whole time?"

Roger shook his head. "Dominick wasn't with me at all. And Linda was kind enough to give me some privacy while I took a leak. But if we go in there and raise hell over a jack-in-the-box, we're going to look really stupid."

"I never intended to raise hell," I said. "We'd just walk back inside and ask who left it. No big deal."

"I say we knock the stupid thing off your car with a stick and then get out of here," Roger suggested. "If the killer did leave it, he wouldn't have been stupid enough to let himself be seen going outside with it, and if we ask too many questions about it we're going to blow the whole reporter setup."

"You're right," I agreed. "But I don't think we should throw it away. It could be an important clue."

"Well, sure, when knives shoot through the sides at us, that'll be an important clue leading us to conclude that it was a trap!"

"Roger, it's a jack-in-the-box! A toy! Nobody knew we were coming! Who the hell keeps explosive knife-shooting jack-in-the-boxes around?"

"Who the hell buries people alive?"

"Okay, look," I said calmly. "It's there for a reason. If our friend wanted us dead, he would have stabbed us to death right after he murdered Jennifer. He would not leave a trap on our car. It's impractical. And unless everyone in Ghoulish Delights is in on it, having us die right outside of the house would immediately get him questioned by the police!"

"Everyone *could* be in on it," said Roger. "They were all pretty scary. That Farley lunatic enjoys his work a little too much, if you ask me."

"Now you're just being ridiculous," I said. "At the very least we need to quit standing around debating this and get out of sight in case somebody comes out to ask us what we're doing. Get in the car. I'll grab the box."

"You're actually going to touch it?"

"Yes."

"Idiot."

"Oh, shut up." I reached for the box...but then hesitated at the last moment. Damn that Roger. Now I was scared to touch a children's toy. The stupid thing couldn't be a trap. There were so many better ways to get rid of us.

"Gee, Andrew, why are you pausing?"

"I told you to get in the car and shut up." I took a deep breath, and slowly extended my index finger toward the box. I made contact, and then pulled back as if I'd just touched a hot stove.

"Something wrong?" asked Roger.

"No, you've got me all freaked out." I forced myself to pick up the jack-in-the-box with both hands, revealing a small piece of paper underneath. Written in blood-red letters were the words "Bad graverobbers!"

This was not good.

I tucked the jack-in-the-box under my arm, picked up the note, and then got in the car. I handed the note to Roger as I set the box in the back seat.

"Oh, piss," said Roger.

"Yep. So, either the killer followed us here, or it's somebody inside."

"Or somebody else could know."

"Right, that too." I started the engine. "We need to find out what's in this box."

"Screw that. I say we take it to the police, let them check it out."

"Roger, are you using your brain on a time-share program?" I asked as I backed out onto the road. "Did you forget that the whole reason we *haven't* gone to the police is that we got into this mess by agreeing to dig up a corpse in the boondocks?"

"We could make something up," said Roger. "Jennifer's dead, it's not like she's gonna contradict us."

I shook my head. "Even if we could come up with a convincing story that answers all the questions they'd throw at us, we don't have anything to give them but a jack-in-the-box. And we don't know what it means yet."

"So what do you suggest we do?"

"Find out what it means."

"I don't know, Andrew, this kind of reminds me of a really nutty decision made by some guys I used to know. They agreed to dig up a coffin for twenty thousand dollars. Where are we going, anyway?"

"To Merriam Lake," I replied. "I might be able to ease your worries."

* * *

"I can't believe we're doing this," said Roger.

I couldn't quite believe it myself. We were parked at the edge of Merriam Lake, standing outside watching the water. The jack-in-the-box had been submerged for the past fifteen minutes. If Roger was so worried that it was going to blow up, I figured we'd dunk it for a while.

I don't know anything about bombs, so I had no idea if this would even do any good. And in fact, I was more inclined to believe that it was really, really dumb. But if it were something low-budget and gunpowder-based, soaking it might work. So that's what I was doing.

Finally I waded out and retrieved the jack-in-the-box. I brought it back to shore and set it down on the grass. "Are you happy now?" I asked.

"No. That couldn't possibly have been enough time to rust any knives in there."

"There aren't any goddamn knives! Do you see any place a knife could come through?" I tapped on the side of the tin box, causing Roger to flinch. "See? Solid. No knives. I'm just going to turn the crank and see what's inside. If you're going to keep being a big baby, you can go hide somewhere and I'll tell you what happened later."

I could tell that the idea was appealing to him, but to his credit Roger stayed where he was. "Okay, I'll watch you turn the crank. Just keep your head away from that top part."

"I was going to." I knelt down beside the box and firmly gripped the handle. I took a deep breath, braced myself, and then let go of the handle. "All right, I don't see any harm in pushing a big mud pile around three of the sides, to sort of block anything that might shoot out, do you?"

Roger agreed that he saw nothing wrong with the idea, so we scooped up some mud from the shore and built a protective barrier around the jack-in-the-box, covering everything but the lid and the handle. That finished, Roger returned to his position of relative safety next to the car and I gripped the handle once more.

I turned the crank. "Pop Goes the Weasel!" began to play. It occurred to me that I didn't know any of the lyrics to this song besides the "Pop Goes the Weasel!" part. I'm sure my brain chose to share that information with me just to distract me from the fact that I was excessively nervous.

Dah-dah, dah-dah, dah-dah-dah-dah-dah, dah-dah, dah-dah, dah-DAH, dah, dah-dah, dah-dah, dah-dah-dah-dah-dah...

I stopped turning right before the weasel went pop.

"Is it broken?" asked Roger.

"No, it's not broken. Leave me alone."

"I'd understand if you want to forget the whole thing."

"Don't talk—you're distracting me."

"From turning the handle?"

"Shut up or I'm yanking this thing right out of the mud and coming after you with it."

"Maybe we should soak it another fifteen minutes."

"No! Just be quiet! I'm going to turn it!" I continued holding the handle, but eased myself as far away from the box as I could and still reach.

Then I turned.

DAH!

Dah-dah-DAH-dah. Dah-dah, dah-dah...

The lousy weasel didn't even know when to pop. I continued turning the handle, and it went through the second verse of "Pop Goes the Weasel," the one that reportedly caused the songwriters to break up over creative differences.

This time, I didn't hesitate at the pop, and the lid sprung open. A cute little clown burst out, bobbing to and fro on his little spring. Taped to one of the clown's hands was a small wet envelope. I tore it off.

"Are you gonna cover that thing with mud, just in case?" Roger asked.

"No, I'm not going to...okay, I'll cover it up to make you feel better." With my foot, I moved a huge glob of mud over the top of the jack-in-the-box. Then, worrying that some kids might come playing around here, I pulled the box out of the mud and heaved it as far into the lake as I could. Nothing blew up and no dead fish rose to the surface, so I figured everything was cool.

I opened the envelope and removed the folded piece of paper inside. Roger apparently decided there was nothing to fear from it and walked over to join me.

On the paper, in the same blood-red letters was written: "If you want to see Jennifer again, be at the Everlife Cemetery at midnight."

"Oh, now *that's* interesting," said Roger.

"That's impossible," I protested. "I heard—"

I stopped. I'd only *heard* her die. It certainly wouldn't be difficult to fake a death that I never got to see.

But why? Why would somebody kidnap Roger, threaten to use him as a hostage but let him go, then fake Jennifer's death, only to use her as a hostage...or something like that?

This whole situation was becoming slightly quaint.

* * *

We were both completely baffled, and so I made the decision for Roger to engage in some real detective work. Meaning that I told him to hide in the woods around the graveyard to see if he could learn the identity of the killer. For some odd reason he was not all that keen on this idea, but using my expert skills at encouraging others to obey my will ("Quit your whining and just do it, for God's sake!"), I managed to convince him. I dropped him off at his apartment with instructions to buy some more bullets for Michael's gun, drive to the cemetery, hide well, and not try to apprehend the killer himself. Not that he ever would.

I drove home to spend some quality minutes with my family before heading out again. Nobody was there, but I saw the light blinking on the answering machine. This pleased me, because Helen had insisted that the new message I'd recorded would cause people to decide they didn't really want us to return their call:

"Hi, you've reached the residence of Andrew, Helen, Theresa, and Kyle Mayhem. Because we've lost a number of close friends lately in telephone-related accidents, we're unable to bring ourselves to answer your call at this time. But if you leave your name and number at the tone, we'll get back to you as soon as therapy cures the problem."

I pressed the button, listened to the message, and immediately got back in my car and drove to the hospital.

CHAPTER NINE

I'm not right very often, but my constant warning of "If you kids don't pick those toys up off the stairs, somebody's going to trip and break their neck!" turned out to be almost true, except that Helen broke her right leg instead.

She was not in a particularly good mood by the time I got there. She was also not all that coherent due to the gobs of medication they'd given her, but I was able to ascertain from her ranting that Kyle's Eye-in-an-Egg had been the culprit.

"I told you not to buy it for him," she snarled. "Didn't I tell you not to buy it for him? Didn't I? We were right there in the store and I said not to buy it, and you went ahead and bought it anyway, you son of a bitch!"

"Yeah, but you said it was stupid, not a health risk," I said, lacking the intelligence not to argue with a drugged-up pissed-off pain-filled woman.

"I don't care. I've always hated that Eye-in-an-Egg, and now because of it I get to spend the next few days in the hospital! Like I don't spend enough time here anyway! I don't see *you* doing all these hours of overtime! Did you get me flowers?"

"Not yet, but I will right away."

"Forget it. I'm going to sleep. Go away."

"I'll make sure that the Eye gets destroyed."

"See that you do."

I left the room and collected my children from our surly-looking neighbor. They were both pretty shaken-up, but I assured them that Mommy was going to be all right and cheered them up by promising them rides on her wheelchair. I made some phone calls, trying to find a place for the kids to stay the night, but nobody was available. I'd try again later. By the time we ate a fast food dinner and got home, it was nearly seven. I wanted to go check on Roger, but I didn't want to risk blowing his cover, or listen to him gripe. Since I really didn't have much time before I wanted to be at Balder's Dash, I decided to simply lie on the couch and try to think things through.

Theresa and Kyle popped in the animated video *Zany the Chipper Chipmunk*. This video always brought out deep feelings of guilt because I wanted so badly to see Zany die. It didn't have to be a gruesome death, just a painful one.

I tried to put the various pieces of the puzzle together, but because I suck as a detective I fell asleep instead. I woke up as Zany was teaching kids the importance of flossing. My leg was being used as the weaponry fort for Kyle's Captain Hocker action figure (with Super-Spitting Action!).

"Grab some stuff to keep you occupied," I said. "Daddy's going to play cards."

* * *

Balder's Dash was meant to be a hangout for college students, but most college students thought it was pretty lame and went elsewhere. As we walked in the door, a movie was playing on a wide-screen TV where some greenish-gray alien was trying to devour some mega-breasted actress while at the same time making sure to jostle her around for maximum bounce. I didn't want my children to witness any more jiggle than absolutely necessary, so we hurried into the back room.

Several people were in there, sitting around a table with about six billion cards spread out in cryptic patterns. Both Carl and Farley were present, and Farley waved as he saw us enter.

"Hey, did you come for your own throat treatment?"

"No, actually I came to learn the game," I said. There was a small couch not being used, so I gave Theresa and Kyle each a kiss and bribed them with Skittles to sit on it and play nicely.

"You came to learn the game?" asked Farley. "I hope you realize this isn't Yahtzee. You're not going to pick up the rules for the first five or six weeks."

"That's fine," I said, pulling up a free chair next to Farley. "By the way, I apologize if I'm just barging in. You guys don't mind if I watch, do you?"

"No, no, we need all the players we can get," Farley assured me. Carl gave me a polite nod, but for the most part kept his eyes glued to the table, obviously planning out some intricate strategy. Introductions were made all around, and then they resumed their game.

I watched carefully for about fifteen minutes without saying anything. This was another case where being Sherlock Holmes might have come in handy, because maybe he would have had some faint comprehension of the rules to this game. One guy, Harold, was sort of the narrator, telling the other players where they were and what demonic beasts were trying to kill them or transform them into minions of evil. That part I got. But whatever they were doing with those cards sounded like complete gibberish.

I was lost. Baffled. Out of my element in society.

Carl set a card down, making the pattern of cards even more hopelessly complex than it already was. "I'll use my Boots of Divine Intervention with an additional three karma points and an additional two stealth points to cross the threshold." He bit his lip nervously as he waited for Harold to roll one of about twenty multi-colored, multi-sided dice. This guy took the game waaaaaay too seriously.

"Fourteen," Harold announced. "What's your Hero rating?"

"Twenty-nine."

"You didn't make it. You fall into the lava storm and lose..." Harold rolled another die, "...seven points from your Health rating."

Carl whitened. "I'll have to use my Cloak of Reconstruction to keep from falling into the Sleep of the Damned!"

"You can't use your cloak," another player pointed out. "It's still cursed for one more turn from my Wand of Dissatisfaction."

"But you're only holding it for six Curse points," said Carl. "So I'm going to use my +3 Reversal Armor to destroy the curse and then I can use my cloak."

"All right," said Harold. "You're currently floating in the lava. Your turn, Farley."

"I'll run down there and get Carl's head for my trophy case. It's time to move up to humans."

"Seriously, Farley, what do you do?"

"How many different points does this game have?" I asked.

"Sixteen points in each of the fields," Farley replied.

"How many fields?"

"There's the Field of Mind, the Field of Body, the Field of Might, the Field of Sorcery, the Field of Destiny, and the Field of Eternity."

"Gotcha. Somehow I missed the Field of Eternity."

"Now, I have a question for you," said Farley. "You're not here to learn the game, and you're not a real reporter. So who are you?"

The other gamers fell silent. Farley's squeaky voice and diminutive stature made him somewhat less than intimidating, but this was still not exactly a development I welcomed.

"What are you talking about?" I asked.

"I can tell by the way you're watching us. You're not watching to see how we play the game—you're trying to study us as individuals. What are you, some kind of FBI agent?"

I was secretly a bit flattered that he might have thought I was FBI material, but I didn't let it go to my head. "Okay, here's the real story. You're right—I'm not here to learn about the game. If I had an extra few hundred I.Q. points I could probably figure out how the hell the rules work, but the truth is that I'm a private investigator."

Carl stared at me, seriously annoyed. "You're disrupting our game because you're a private investigator?"

"That's right."

Farley's face lit up with fascination. "That is so cool! Which one of us are you investigating? It's Rachel, right? I always knew she was up to something shady."

"No, I'm here because your friend Michael Ashcraft has turned up missing. His wife hired me to find out where he is."

"Mike's missing?" asked Carl. "For how long?"

"Wasn't Michael Ashcraft that guy who stayed here for

about ten minutes then called us all a bunch of geeks and stormed out?" asked Harold.

"He's been gone since last night," I told Carl. "The police won't help because he hasn't been missing for twenty-four hours, but his wife believes there may be some element of foul play."

"Wasn't he on vacation?" Carl asked.

"It fell through," I said.

Farley pushed back his chair and jumped to his feet. "I know who it was!" he announced, and then pointed at Carl. "It was you! You had the motive, means, and opportunity! You've always hated Michael because his mother liked him better than your mother liked you! It was you! Admit it!"

"Sit down, you little nerd," Carl muttered.

Farley's eyes widened as he pretended to have another shocking realization. "But wait! It could also have been...me! That's right! How silly of me not to think of it in the first place! I'm the one who followed Michael home last night, burst into his living room, beat him to death with a snow globe, chopped up his body with a set of Ginsu knives, then stuffed the evidence down the garbage disposal, following it with a slice of lemon to disguise the smell. That's it! I've done your work for you, Andrew Mayhem...if that *is* your name!"

"Yeah, that's my name. Look, I didn't come here to interrupt your game, but do you and Carl mind if I ask you guys some questions?"

Carl looked pained at the idea of leaving the game, but Farley nodded enthusiastically. "Sure, anything to help a private eye. By the way, how much do you guys make?"

"Millions," I said. "Movie stars get the fame, but we get the cash. How about I talk to you first, then Carl after we're done?"

"Fine by me," said Farley. He gestured toward the side of the room where Theresa and Kyle were playing. "Step into my office."

Theresa was sitting on a beanbag, so I sat down on the couch then hoisted Kyle up on my lap. Farley sat down next to us. "Have you ever shot anyone?" he asked.

Kyle looked up at me. "Have you, Daddy?"

"No, I've never shot anyone. That's all TV stuff. Most of a private investigator's work is really boring." I think I'd read that somewhere.

"Yeah, but do you take pictures of people cheating on their wives and husbands and bosses and that kind of thing?"

"I'm trying to get out of that field," I said. "Sometimes the emotions involved are just too intense. So tell me about Michael."

"You mean, does he have any enemies?"

"That would be a good place to start, yeah."

"I don't know if he has any enemies or not. I hardly ever see him outside of work. His wife's a babe, though, don't you think?"

"Kyle, why don't you go over and play with Theresa?" I suggested.

"I want to hear about the babe."

"Kyle, go play with Theresa."

Kyle reluctantly slid off my lap and went over to torment his sister. "Do you see Jennifer much?" I asked.

"You mean, do I see much of Jennifer?" Farley chuckled. The sleazy attitude seemed out of place coming from this little twerp. "Nah. She comes around sometimes and complains that Mike should be spending more time at home instead of at work, but that's about it. Most of us just ignore her. Especially Rachel, she can't stand her."

"I got that impression. Now, let me ask you kind of a strange question. If Michael had a safety deposit box, what would you say might be in it?"

"Is that the kind of question they train you to ask in private investigator academy?"

"Just work with me. What might be inside?"

"I have no idea. Maybe nude pictures of his wife."

"Do you know if he had any money stored away?"

"Nope. The only time money came into conversation was when he said we were spending too much on the videos. So do you have to take a test to become a private eye or can anyone do it?"

"A written test, and a psychological screening," I replied. "At least in Florida." That sounded good.

"Do you get to carry a gun?"

"Yes, but I usually don't."

"Why not?"

"I don't need one. Like I said, it's usually boring. Did

Michael and Jennifer ever fight when they were around you guys?"

"You think she did something to him?"

"It's just a question."

Farley hesitated. "Can this be off the record?"

"Absolutely."

"I think she's cheating on him. Mike is paranoid beyond belief, but this is one thing he may have been right about."

"Did he accuse her?"

"No, nothing blatant, at least not that I know about. But you could tell he didn't like having any of us around her. And when they were together, you could tell something was up."

"How could you tell?" I asked.

"I don't know—you're the one who's familiar with psychological testing. All I can say is that if you're going to keep asking around, that may be something to bring up."

"Thanks," I said. "That'll be helpful."

"So do the cops resent you for intruding upon their turf?"

"No."

"Do you think I could tag along with you one day, on a stakeout or something? I won't get in the way."

"Don't you already have a career in special effects?"

"I don't want to change careers, I just want to see what it's like to be a gumshoe. What kind of car do you drive?"

"A ratty old gray one."

"To be inconspicuous, right?"

"You know it."

"That is *so* cool. Hey, if you need anything else, feel free to ask. I'll go get Carl for you, if I can drag his obsessed butt away from the game."

"Thanks."

As Farley returned to the table I tried to figure out what to do with that new piece of information. Could Jennifer be behind this whole thing? If so, who was her accomplice with the knife? And once again, why?

Carl came over and sat down on the couch. "Do you think Mike's okay?" he asked.

"That's what I'm trying to find out. When was the last time you saw him?" This was a pretty obvious question that I should have asked Farley, but I didn't think of it due to the previously stated fact that I suck as a detective.

"Last week. He was all psyched about going to Europe."

"Was Jennifer with him?"

Carl nodded. "She picked him up at work."

"Did she come inside?"

"Just to tell him to hurry up."

"Do you think they're a happy couple?"

Carl shrugged. "Sure."

"What makes you think so?"

Carl looked uncomfortable. "I don't know, why shouldn't they be? Isn't Jennifer the one who hired you?"

"Yes, she is. I'm just trying to find out everything I can. Do you think she was faithful to him?"

"How should I know? She never asked me to videotape her sleeping around or anything, if that's what you're wondering."

"No, that's not quite what I was wondering, but thanks. Now here's a fill-in-the-blank question: If Michael owned a safety deposit box, it would contain what?"

Carl looked very confused. "Huh?"

I was giving serious consideration to dropping this question from future interrogations. "Just say the first thing that pops into your mind."

"Nothing pops into my mind." He thought for a moment. "Legal documents, backup copies of software programs, I don't know. Why are you asking?"

"Like I said, just getting information."

"I don't think I have any information. All I do is videotape stuff for Ghoulish Delights and occasionally help them with the new scenarios. Can I get back to the game?"

"Sure, have fun. Slay an elf for me."

"My character *is* an elf!"

I gathered up my children and we headed back into the main area. That same alien was trying to devour another actress who wore nothing to block Kyle's view of her jiggling capabilities, so I covered his eyes with my hand and led him outside.

We walked a block to an outdoor pay phone and I began to make more calls. My in-laws still weren't home, nor were either of the babysitters who hadn't blacklisted my children. "It's Thursday night, where on earth *are* these people?" I asked aloud.

"When can we see Mommy?" asked Theresa.

"Not until visiting hours start tomorrow," I said. "But we'll call her as soon as I find a babysitter."

"We don't need a babysitter," Theresa insisted. "I can watch Kyle."

"No, you can't!" said Kyle.

"Forget it, there's no way in the world I'm leaving you two alone," I said. "I'd come back and the house would have sunk like the Titanic. Who's that one lady who watched you that one time? The lady with that stupid dog with those foofy things on its tail?"

"Mrs. Denkle," said Theresa. "She moved."

"Is she still in Florida?"

"Maybe."

I decided I wasn't going to spend the rest of the evening chasing around a Mrs. Denkle who might still live in Florida. I made a couple more desperate phone calls, but came up empty. So the only person left to watch them was currently hiding out in a cemetery. Great.

I called Helen at the hospital and let the kids talk to her for two minutes each. Then I told her that the kids and I planned to spend the rest of the evening at home watching television. This wasn't the truth, and my lie would be probably be revealed the very next time she spoke with our children, but for now it was worth it just to keep Helen from worrying.

It was about nine o'clock. I herded the kids into the car and we drove the twenty minutes to the Everlife Cemetery. It was a large cemetery with no gates surrounding it. Though there were no hills, a couple of large mausoleums provided an excellent place to hide, along with the bordering woods.

"Okay, we're going to play a new game," I said. "It's called Car Hide and Seek. I want both of you to duck down as far as you can and hide. I'm going to step right outside the car, and when I get back in I'll see if I can find you. How does that sound?"

"That's silly, Daddy," Theresa informed me.

"But silly games are the most fun, right?"

"No."

"Yeah!" said Kyle, most likely just to contradict her.

"Play Daddy's silly game and we'll play another game later. Now duck down. I don't want to be able to see any part of you when I'm outside the car."

They both squished down as far as they could, and I got out of the car. Since I was here almost three hours early, I didn't really expect the killer to be around anyway, but I wanted to take as few chances as possible.

"Roger! Hey, Roger! It's Andrew! You awake?"

A moment later I saw Roger step out from behind some trees at the far end of the cemetery. As he began to crutch toward me, I could see that he didn't look happy. Not that I blamed him.

"What's up?" he called out.

"Change of plans. I couldn't get rid of the kids."

"You mean I sat out here all this time for nothing?"

"Yep. Did you see anything?"

"Not a thing. You brought me food, right?"

"Uh, yeah, I think Kyle still has all of his green Skittles left."

"You suck, man." Roger reached me, slightly out of breath and covered with sweat and dirt. "So what are we supposed to do now?"

"My guess is that you don't want to hang out here another few hours and meet our friend yourself, right?"

"Good guess."

"So we'll trade." I glanced back at the car to make sure the kids weren't peeking. "Hand over the flashlight."

He handed it to me.

"Take the kids to your place," I said. "I want them in bed by ten, and no sugar unless you absolutely can't get them to go to bed without it. Where's your car?"

"It's parked at a church about two miles away. Just follow the road that way," Roger said, pointing. "Enjoy the fact that you're not doing it on crutches."

"Thanks. I guess I'll get in touch with you later. Try and keep the phone line free, okay?"

"Are you sure you want to do this? There's no law saying you have to show up here just because some psycho killer left a message in a jack-in-the-box."

"Don't worry, I'll be careful," I assured him.

After we traded keys, I opened the car door, located my children, and gave them the usual instructions about not driving Roger to the brink of suicide. Then they left, and I headed for the cover of woods to wait.

CHAPTER TEN

Three hours waiting in a graveyard after dark starts to get to you. I don't know why. Maybe it's all the dead people hanging around underground. Whatever it was, by the time my watch said it was ten minutes to midnight, I had a major case of the creeps, the willies, and the heebie-jeebies. At least the flesh-eating zombies were keeping themselves hidden away.

I sat there for another ten minutes and the same nothing that had been happening all night continued happening. I wondered if the killer was hiding someplace else, waiting for me to drive by. Maybe without somebody acting as bait (which was to be my job in the original plan), he wouldn't show up. Regardless, I was going to wait at least another half hour before I gave up.

Then I heard a faint beeping, like an alarm clock going off. For a moment I thought it was my creeped-out, willied, and heebie-jeebied imagination, but a few more seconds convinced me that, yes, I was definitely hearing a beeping. You weren't generally supposed to hear beeping in a cemetery at midnight, so I had a pretty good idea that this had something to do with the reason I was here.

I surveyed as much of the graveyard as I could see, which was most of it. Nobody around. The killer could have left a beeper any time before our stakeout, maybe even before Jennifer hired us.

Reluctantly I emerged from my hiding spot, turned on the flashlight, and began to walk toward the beeping sound. It was hard to gauge exactly where it was coming from, but after a couple of minutes I pinpointed the spot and knelt down beside a small hole in the ground, about the size of a dime.

I stuck my finger in the hole and pulled away dirt until I'd revealed a small kitchen timer. I shut it off, and then removed the note that was taped to it. Once again, the same blood-red letters. "Find Jennifer Where You Find Love."

What was that supposed to mean? Find Jennifer where you find love? What was it, singles night at the Everlife Cemetery? Had I really sat around for three hours waiting for this?

Okay, stop it, I told myself. It obviously means something. Be a non-sucky detective. Get that brain into gear. Find Jennifer where you find love. Find Jennifer where you find love.

Love. My heart gave a jolt as I suddenly wondered if they'd involved Helen, but that was ridiculous. The killer certainly hadn't stashed Jennifer under her hospital bed.

Was I supposed to find love here, in the cemetery? This was entering some really sick territory.

Lovers buried together? That was a possibility, but there had to be dozens of them around. Something left by a lover? Once again, there could be dozens of them. But hey, maybe the killer just wasn't any good at narrowing things down. It was worth looking.

I began to wander up and down the rows of tombstones, shining my flashlight on each one. Wherever I found flowers, I poked through them, but found nothing interesting. This was going to take forever.

And then I had a sudden brainstorm. There may not be many people around with the last name "Mayhem," but there were plenty with the last name "Love."

I picked up my pace, looking only at the names. Five minutes later, I stopped at a pair of small, cracked tombstones. Timothy and Karen Love. Both of them 1892-1954. "Died in each other's arms."

There was a basket of flowers resting in front of the tombstone. If this was wrong, I was going to feel like a total creep, but nevertheless I turned the basket over and shook it until something fell out. A picture in a frame. It was not a nice picture. It was a picture of a woman screaming. Not Jennifer. I actually thought I recognized her, an actress from some zero-budget horror films. The picture was probably a shot from one of her movies. The interesting part was the frame. It was one of those frames with a little speaker inside, so you can record a short message. It was intended to be something like "I'm thinking about you" or "You're always in my heart." I suspected that the message here was going to be something quite different.

I pressed the button and was treated to the sound of a female shriek, followed by some maniacal laughter that sounded like it had been generated from a computer. Then a sound bite that I recognized from *The Exorcist*, a demonic voice proclaiming "This sow is mine!"

A chorus of children: "You're gonna diiiiie, you're gonna diiiiie."

A musical sting, the kind you hear right as the monster bursts out of nowhere.

An old man speaking in a careful, calculated tone: "True horror exists deep beneath the surface."

Another female shriek.

A hysterical man: "Blood! Blood everywhere! It covers the walls! It covers the ceiling!"

The *Twilight Zone* theme.

A whisper: "Look beneath...look within..."

The recording ended.

It took me several seconds to remember to breathe. Sweat was pouring down my sides, and I was getting the kind of headache I always got before a really difficult test in college.

"It's nothing," I said aloud. "Just some guy with a bit of a twist in his personality trying to mess with my mind, that's all."

"*DIE DIE DIE DIE DIE DIE!!!*"

I dropped the picture in shock, and then willed my stomach to untangle itself from my spinal column. Just a little bonus sound bite, like the hidden tracks you can find on some CDs. Nothing to keel over dead from.

But I also had nothing to go on.

Okay, "true horror exists beneath the surface" was probably a clue. I didn't like that clue, because it implied that I was going to have to dig up another grave, and I was trying to cut down. But where? The Love's site certainly didn't look like anything had been added to it recently. Was I going to have to wander around, shining my flashlight all over until I found a patch of ground that looked recently-filled?

"Look beneath...look within..."

It had to refer to digging up another grave. Or else the tombstones of Mr. Beneath and Mr. Within. The only other thing I could look beneath was the picture.

I picked up the frame, half expecting it to tell me to DIE! DIE! DIE! again. I removed the picture and found another note behind it.

"Good guess. But wrong."

What a prick.

Okay, fine, it wasn't behind the picture. Where else was I supposed to look? I wandered around the nearby tombstones, searching for an area that might have something newly-buried underneath it, but there was nothing.

Maybe I was supposed to smash open the picture frame.

I turned it over. Better idea. Look in the battery compartment.

I pried open the compartment and saw four tiny batteries.

Then one of the batteries fell out, revealing a very small, folded piece of paper. I unfolded it and letters I could barely even see spelled out "OLE."

Ole? Spanish for "Bravo?" What was this, congratulations for not going absolutely berserk up to this point?

I shook the frame and the other batteries dropped out. Three more pieces of paper fell to the ground. After I retrieved and unfolded them, I had the following fragments: "US," "MA," and "UM."

Great. Another puzzle. And I was the kind of person who cheated at Scrabble.

"Us" and "Ma" could refer to people, I guess, but what were "Um" and "Ole" supposed to mean? Was I supposed to be searching for a Mexican couple who lived with their mother and used verbal tags?

Maybe these could be unscrambled to form another name. No! I had it!

With a little rearranging the fragments formed ... MAU-
SOLEUM.

I headed over to the closest mausoleum, which was also
the larger of the two. The door was chained shut with a shiny
new padlock, but when I walked around to the back there
was a patch of earth, about as long as a coffin, that, while
firmly packed, could easily have been replaced recently.

Jennifer could be down there.

If so, she'd probably been there since last night.

This was not going to be pretty.

Now I decided that the best course of action was to run to
the car, drive to the nearest phone, and get the police. If Jennifer was buried alive, every second might count, and I wasn't
going to get very far trying to dig with my bare hands. But I
took a moment to shine my flashlight around the area, just
in case I'd missed something, and there it was. Another one
of those notes, taped to the mausoleum wall near the ground.
I tore it free and read it. "13 left, 27 right, 4 left."

I hurried to the front of the mausoleum and turned the dial
of the padlock to that combination. It popped open, and I threw
it aside. I pulled open the heavy wooden door, shined the flashlight inside, and immediately saw what I was supposed to find.
Two shovels. A lantern. A Walkman. And yes, a note.

"Dig her up yourselves or suffer the consequences," the
note read. "But you may want to hurry."

I grabbed one of the shovels, the lantern, and the Walkman
and rushed to the back of the mausoleum. Opening the
Walkman, I saw that the tape inside was labeled "Music To
Dig Up Graves By." Oh, yes, this guy was certainly a prick.

I spent the next half hour digging as rapidly as I could. I
kept the Walkman volume low so that I could hear if anyone
approached, but I got to listen to songs like "Digging in the
Dirt" by Peter Gabriel, Perry Como singing "Dig You Later,"
Randy Travis singing "Digging Up Bones," They Might Be Gi-
ants singing "Dig My Grave," and "Dirty Deeds Done Dirt
Cheap" by AC/DC.

Then I struck coffin.

I quickly removed more dirt until the lid was exposed
enough that I could open it. This was made a bit more difficult because I was trying to keep myself in a position where I
wouldn't get shot if bullets started firing through the lid.

I knocked on the lid with the shovel. "Jennifer?"

Silence.

I could think of so many things I'd rather do than open this coffin. Root canals, alligator wrestling, parent-teacher conferences...bring 'em on!

But I got the shovel in place, and then pried it open.

There was not a corpse inside.

There wasn't a live body inside, either.

The only thing inside the coffin was a video camera.

Great. I'd spontaneously generated six ulcers over a stupid video camera. I picked it up, and then shut the lid. It was an older model, heavy and clunky. Probably not something that would be missed if it were taken out of the Ghoulish Delights office.

I sat down against the wall of the mausoleum and examined the camcorder more thoroughly. I ejected the tape inside and saw that it was labeled "You'll like this." I stuck the tape back in, and then unplugged the headphones from the Walkman and inserted them into the headphone jack of the video recorder. I peered through the viewfinder and pressed "play."

A black-and-white image appeared. It was Jennifer, her hair much longer than when I'd met her. She wore a black leather outfit and high heels. As she walked onto the empty stage, the camera zoomed in on her face, and she gave a spank-me-you-bad-boy smile.

"Welcome to *Ghoulish Delights*," she said, sounding like she was on a commercial for a 1-900-DO-ME-NOW line. "I'm sure you'll looooove what we've got in store for you. But before we get to the good stuff, let's hear a word from our sponsor, Profit Jewelers. You know, nose rings, lip rings, navel rings, and a wide variety of other piercings are the fashion right now, but Profit Jewelers, always the innovator, has taken things one step further."

The camera panned over to where a woman I didn't recognize sat on a chair, smiling broadly and waving at the camera like a professional model. She was very attractive except for the ring protruding from her left eyeball.

"Yes, eye rings," said Jennifer. "They're what all the top stars are wearing, and as an extra-special bonus, they huuuuuurt when they go in." She purred these last words, but for some reason I still wasn't convinced to go get my eye pierced.

She began to scratch her back. "Don't you hate that one little spot on your back that you can never seem to reach? Usually somebody is here to scratch it for me." She made this sound like one of the most erotic acts imaginable. "But tonight I'm on my own, so I'll have to improvise."

Jennifer ripped off her left arm in a spray of blood, and then used it to scratch her back. Even with a one-inch, grainy black-and-white picture it wasn't a very convincing special effect.

"That's soooo much better," she told the camera. She tossed the arm off-screen. After a series of loud chewing sounds, a skeletal arm was tossed back to her. "Now, before we get to our main attraction, it's time once again for Cooking With Chef Pierre."

The camera followed her as she walked over to an oven, upon which rested a large metal pot. A man who had obviously been dead for quite some time was standing by the oven, tied to a pole so he wouldn't topple over. "This is Chef Pierre," Jennifer explained. "Master of culinary treats. So, what have you got for us today?"

Steam poured up into her face as she removed the lid. She inhaled deeply, and sighed with pleasure. "Ooooh, my favorite. Now, this creation is for those who love spaghetti, but don't find it quite hearty enough." She dipped out a spoonful of the contents. Intestines.

"I wonder if it's done?" Jennifer grabbed a foot-long segment of the intestine and flung it against the wall. It stuck. "Ah! Perfect!"

I shifted my position, wondering what I was supposed to be getting out of this. Maybe they wanted me to promote a new restaurant.

"And now, it's time for our feature presentation," said Jennifer. "His name is...well, you don't really need to know his name to enjoy it, so here we go!"

The scene switched to a bedroom. There was a young man on the bed, maybe in his mid-twenties, wearing only a pair of boxer shorts. He'd been tied there, spread eagle, a gag over his mouth. The camera zoomed in close on his face, revealing eyes wide with terror. If this guy was an actor, he was good. But I didn't think he was an actor.

The camera pulled back from his face, and then began to circle him as the person taping this walked to the other side of the bed. The man watched it the entire time. There was no sound, but you could tell he was whimpering.

Then the camera operator's gloved hand came into the frame, holding a pocket knife. It was opened to a spork.

I pressed the fast-forward button just as the camera operator went to work on the man's upper leg. For nearly five minutes I watched what was happening, and even in speeded-up motion on the tiny screen it made me violently queasy. The spork was not the only tool used. The corkscrew was especially grisly.

I wanted to believe that it was all just special effects, but I knew that it wasn't. It was all one continuous shot, with no opportunities to replace the live actor with a Karo syrup-filled dummy. And when the pocketknife was upgraded to a hatchet, the man flailed around too much for his missing right arm to have been simply tucked out of sight.

No actor could maintain that level of terror and agony for so long.

This was real.

I took it off fast-forward as the man was finally allowed to die. The gloved hand, now drenched with blood, gave a thumbs-up sign to the camera. The screen faded to black.

Jennifer reappeared, smiling mischievously. "Ooooh, that *had* to hurt, don't you think? That's all for this episode, but let's see some coming attractions."

The picture cut to a young woman tied to a chair. The scene shifted four more times, showing two other women and two men, all tied up and ripe for the torturing. Then the scene returned to Jennifer.

"I hope you've enjoyed Ghoulish Delights, and I hope you'll come see us again some time."

She blew a kiss at the camera, then ran her tongue over her upper lip as the picture faded out.

I fast-forwarded to the end, but there was nothing else on the tape.

Now what?

That was an easy one to answer. I was going straight to the police.

CHAPTER ELEVEN

I didn't bother to rebury the coffin. Screw it. The cops were going to get the full story. The whole situation had been out of control before, but now it was too much for me to handle. Let the police deal with the lunatic making snuff films. This stretched well beyond the death of Michael Ashcraft, and I was done with it.

I walked along the side of the road at a brisk pace, the video camera tucked under my arm. No cars passed as I made my way to the church where Roger had parked. I half-expected The Apparition to show up and offer me another lift. It had been that kind of bizarre evening.

The flashlight battery died about halfway there, forcing me to walk in total darkness. I found it hard to be surprised.

I got in the car and took a couple of minutes to compose myself before I started the engine. I didn't want to get in a wreck and leave my kids with two parents in the hospital, or one in the morgue.

I pulled onto the road and searched the AM radio stations until I found the easiest listening music on the dial. I needed a station that would advertise itself as "Music for the aging, comatose kind of guy." My nerves were in desperate need of soothing. I thanked God I'd never tried drugs, or this would have sent me into an acid flashback for sure.

I let the music calm me down for about two minutes.

Then a phone rang.

Roger didn't own a cellular phone. Unless he'd bought one within the past couple of days and forgot to mention it, I had a pretty strong suspicion that this was not going to be a call I wanted to hear.

The phone rang again. It wasn't difficult to locate, wedged between the front seats. I picked it up, noting that it looked just like the one Jennifer had given me, extended the antenna, and answered. "Hello?"

"Having fun?"

It was a very low, computer-generated voice, spoken in a monotone. Apparently the killer had one of those voice disguiser gizmos after all.

"Who is this?" I demanded.

For a few seconds I could only hear a faint clicking, as if somebody was typing on a keyboard. Then the voice again: "I'm the villain in your life story."

"Listen to me, you deviant freak, I'm not playing your game anymore. As soon as I hang up on your sorry ass I'm calling the police."

"Oh, don't do that. That's no fun."

"No, fun is taking my kids to an amusement park. Fun is not spending all night at a graveyard so I can dig up a coffin with a tape of *America's Most Fucked-Up Home Videos*!"

"You just don't know how to party."

"I'm hanging up now."

"I wouldn't."

"Why not?"

"People will die."

"Who?"

"You'll find out."

"I'm not playing around any more," I said. "Tell me who this is. Is this Jennifer?"

"Maybe."

"Okay, fine, I don't expect you to reveal your secret identity. Tell me why you're doing this."

"I have nothing to loss."

"What the hell does 'nothing to loss' mean? What was that, a typo?"

Silence.

"Jeez, Mr. or Mrs. Psychopathic Dipshit, you'd think if

you were going to go to all the trouble of letting your computer do the talking you'd be more careful with your typing so you wouldn't sound like a complete moron."

Still no response.

"What's the matter, did you loss your voice?"

"It won't seem so funny when you're the one tied to that bed." It was the computer speaking. I'd hoped to make the killer mad enough to break in on the conversation, but no such luck.

"No, you're right, it probably won't," I conceded. "That's why I'm not giving it a chance to happen."

"People will die."

"You already said that. Are you using macros now?"

The typing grew louder and faster. "You listen to me, Andrew Mayhem. I have five people locked away who are going to die the same excruciating death you saw tonight if you don't follow my instructions."

"Yeah, right. How do I know you're not bluffing, like you did when you said you were going to keep Roger?"

"You'll get the tapes."

"Uh-huh. Sure."

"Don't push it, Mayhem. If I have to, I'll bring one of them down right now and you can listen to me rip her apart. Did you watch the tape all the way through?"

"Yeah."

"Then you know which five people I'm talking about."

It still could have been a bluff, but after seeing the tape, and after possibly hearing Jennifer stabbed to death last night, I decided it wasn't worth taking a chance. "Fine. You've got my attention. What's up?"

"I wanted to tell you that you're doing well."

"Really? Wow, you just don't know how much your approval means to me. My parents never thought I'd amount to anything, and hearing your words of encouragement has really brightened my night. Thank you so very the hell much."

A loud honk made me realize that I had drifted into the opposite lane and was heading toward a Volkswagen. I quickly jerked the steering wheel and got back where I belonged.

"You should be more careful," the killer's computer informed me.

"Chew me."

"Here are the rules, Andrew. Do not talk about what has happened. If you tell anyone, those five innocent people will die horribly. If you keep quiet and play along, they will be released. Do you understand?"

"When will they be released?" I asked.

"Soon."

"That doesn't cut it. Tell me exactly when they'll be released and maybe we've got a deal."

"Very soon. That's all I can say."

"All right. I won't talk to anyone."

"Good. But I want you to keep investigating. Learn all you can. Try to find out who I am. Play the game. Have fun with it."

"I don't see any potential for fun here, but I'll do my best. So why are you doing this? If you're some freakazoid who gets off on torturing people, that's your business, but why am I involved?"

"Soon it's going to be all over for me. As I said, I have nothing to lose. I'm going to die, and I want to be remembered for something big. I'm giving you the adventure of a lifetime so you'll make sure everyone else remembers me."

"Hell, if you quit right now I'll hire a skywriter."

"No, I don't want to quit before the real fun begins. Would you like a clue about who I am?"

"By all means."

"I'm not Jennifer."

"Well, I'll be sure to scratch her off my list of suspects."

"I want you to see her again. Not on video, in the flesh. Maybe you can save her."

"So she isn't dead?"

"Not necessarily. Pull over and stop the car. Make it someplace abandoned. Then tell me where you are, and I'll help you find her."

I pulled into the parking lot of a strip mall, and then drove behind the buildings. I stopped next to a garbage dumpster and shut off the engine. "Okay, I'm parked."

"Where are you?"

"Don't you know? I assumed you had helicopter surveillance or something."

"Do you want to find her or not?"

"I'm behind the Parnola mall."

"Much better. You picked a good place. She's very close. Now here's the game. There are five quarters hidden in Roger's car. Each one has a different date. In ten minutes, I'm going to call you back, and you're going to tell me all five of the dates."

"And what's the penalty in this little game?"

"Death. For each quarter you miss, one of the prisoners dies."

Like I needed any more pressure. "You said they'd be released if I kept quiet!"

"No, I said you had to play along. So play along. Jennifer will help you."

The killer hung up. I cursed loudly in multiple quantities, and then checked my watch. 1:47 A.M. Okay, fine, I'd play along. How hard could it be to find some quarters?

I turned on the overhead light, then did a quick visual search of the front and back seat and saw nothing. I pulled down each of the sun visors in case quarters were taped to them, but no luck. I opened the glove compartment and two half-empty bottles of aspirin fell out, along with a woman's severed hand.

"Oh, shit!" I screamed, recoiling against the driver's side door to get away from it. The hand rested on the floor, palm down. Some specks of blood had dried on the wedding ring.

I sat there for a moment, unable to move. Okay, get over it, I finally told myself. If you sit here trembling some people will die. Find those quarters.

I thought I'd caught a glimpse of silver as the hand fell, so I reached over with my foot and used the toe of my shoe to flip it over. In the palm rested a quarter. I tried to slide it off, but it was clearly glued on. I leaned down to get a closer look. Tails. To see the date, I was going to have to pull it off.

There was absolutely no time for squeamishness, so I ripped the quarter off and placed it on the seat. A tiny piece of flesh came off with the quarter, but I put that way the hell out of my mind and rummaged through the glove compartment until I'd searched it completely. No other quarters.

Under the seat was a good possibility.

Not that I'd be able to see where I was reaching.

Oh, I could think of so many things I'd rather be doing.

Still using my foot, I pushed the hand as far out of the

way as possible, then leaned down and tried to look underneath the passenger seat. I couldn't see a thing.

I reached underneath, moving my hand slowly, praying I wouldn't find any more of Jennifer. The thought that the killer might have placed something like a mousetrap under the seat also occurred to me, in case the first thought hadn't been bad enough.

My hand slid against something wet.

I nearly tore the skin off my fingers in my haste to yank my hand out of there, and I nearly bit my tongue off in my effort not to shriek.

Doing my best to ignore the scarlet streak on the side of my hand, I checked my watch. Two minutes had already passed. I had to get over my reluctance and find those quarters right away. I could always find a nice comfy padded cell later.

I reached back underneath the seat, wishing that I were a boring, unimaginative person who was unable to visualize all the possibilities for what my hand was exploring.

Then I let out a small yelp as something bit me.

After yanking my hand free once again, I realized my mistake. It hadn't been a bite. I'd just poked myself on something—a protruding bone, most likely.

If there wasn't a quarter underneath the seat after all this, I was going to be seriously irked.

Once again I began the search. I felt my way around for a full minute before locating the quarter, which was hidden way in the back. I pulled my arm out and resisted the urge to wipe my hand on Roger's upholstery.

I moved to the other side and reached underneath the passenger seat. My hand made contact with something, and this time it was easy to identify. A foot. Two feet, actually, as I discovered when I moved my hand to the right. This wasn't nearly as bad as whatever had been under the other seat, and I found the quarter wedged between the little piggy who had none and the little piggy who went wee wee wee all the way home.

I looked at my watch again and realized that this had taken longer than I thought. Only four minutes left.

Okay, there was a definite motif here, so the quarters could only be hidden someplace large enough to hide a body part. The trunk was a logical place to check. I pulled the trunk release, got out of the car, and lifted the lid.

It was filled to the top with confetti.

Without hesitation, I thrust my hands inside and began searching through it as rapidly as I could. I found the spare tire right away, but shortly after that my hand brushed against some hair. Long hair. I grabbed a fistful of it and lifted Jennifer's severed head out of the confetti.

I couldn't let the fact that I was holding a head distract me. I turned it all around, searching for a quarter that might be glued to it. Nothing. I ran my fingers all through her hair, and found nothing there, either. I checked the ears, in case it were some demented variation of the magic trick my uncle always liked to show me, but that was also unsuccessful.

A possible hiding spot occurred to me.

I shook the head violently, trying to jar loose anything that might be in its mouth. Nothing fell out.

It looked like I was going to find out how long it took a dead tongue to dry out, after all.

I reached inside her mouth. I can't describe what it felt like, because my hand went completely numb. But I quickly found the quarter, underneath her tongue. It had been wrapped in cellophane, which was nailed down to keep it in place. I tore it free, dropped the head back in the confetti, and shut the trunk.

Four out of five. The fifth one was probably either under the car or under the front hood. I hurried back to the front seat to pop open the hood.

The phone rang.

I quickly scooped up the quarters I'd placed on the seat and picked up the phone. It rang again, but I didn't answer. I pulled the lever to open the hood, then ran to the front of the car and lifted the hood.

Nothing looked unusual. The phone continued to ring.

Damn it! I couldn't answer, or the killer would know that I only found four of the quarters. But if I didn't answer, all five of the prisoners might die!

I answered. "Yeah?"

"Did you meet Jennifer?" It was the same computer-generated monotone.

"Oh, yeah. That was real clever." I frantically began lifting hoses and looking anywhere a body part might be hidden.

"What's your honest opinion? Can she be saved?"

"Screw you." I had no time for wit.

"Tell me the dates on the quarters. You have ten seconds."

I tried to make my voice as casual as possible. "1994, 1980, 2001, 1976, and 1997."

There was a long pause on the other end, longer than the normal pauses for typing. "Not bad. Four out of five."

"What do you mean, four out of five? I found them all!"

"Only four were correct. So, Andrew, I'll be a sport and let you pick who's going to die. If you need to review the tape, feel free."

"Hell no! Now, you listen to me. I'm willing to play along with your game, but you have to stick with the rules you set up! If I found all five quarters, all five people get to live, and if you're not going to honor that I'll be talking to the cops before you can say 'I'm a psychotic asshole.'"

"There was no 1997 quarter."

"The hell there wasn't! I found one quarter in the glove compartment, one quarter under each seat, one quarter in the trunk, and one quarter wedged in the seat cushion in the back. That's five. If you disagree, get your ass back to elementary school."

"There wasn't one in the back."

"There most certainly *was* one in the back. Hey, maybe the quarter was already there, but if you were dumb enough to pick something that could have been in the car before you started, that's not my fault. I can't help it if you didn't check out the car thoroughly. Once I found the five quarters, I quit."

There was a very long pause before the computer voice spoke.

"You're a lying bastard, Andrew."

I didn't respond. I just stood there, cringing.

"But I'm going to give you points for effort. None of the prisoners will die tonight."

I was astonished, but I certainly wasn't going to let it show. "So now what?"

"If you need to, get yourself cleaned up. If you didn't already find it, there's a towel and some rubbing alcohol on the left side of the trunk, under the confetti. Leave the car. It will be taken care of. A cab will meet you out front."

"And after that?"

"Try and find me. But remember what I said about not talking to anyone about tonight. And no cops. If the police come after me, I'll have plenty of warning time to kill the prisoners, and make it hurt. I could be anyone, so watch yourself. And like I said, have fun."

"My joy sensors are going into overload already."

"But make sure you get in that cab, or I'll have to make a new video. Good night, Andrew. I'll be in touch."

The killer hung up.

I didn't know what else to do. I opened the trunk again, got as much of the blood off as possible, and went out front to wait for the taxi.

* * *

"What happened to you?" asked Roger as he opened the door to his apartment.

"It was bad. Real bad." I stepped inside and saw Theresa and Kyle sleeping safely on the pullout bed. Until this whole thing was resolved, it was going to be difficult to let them out of my sight.

Now I was sort of in a bind. Could I tell Roger about the horrors of last night? For all I knew, the place could be bugged. The phone could be tapped. I didn't know what kind of resources the killer had, and honestly I didn't know enough about surveillance to know what degree of paranoia was justified. At the moment I was envisioning some eccentric billionaire with cameras hidden in every corner of Chamber, sitting in his cushioned chair in a room with five hundred monitors, stroking his ugly cat.

So I didn't want to say anything to Roger. What good would it do, anyway? He'd end up an even more reluctant partner than he already was. Nah, I'd shield him from the hard stuff for the time being.

"I can't talk about it," I said. "I will say that I'm not entirely certain you're ever going to get your car back."

"I beg your pardon?"

"It's either being cleaned or incinerated—I'm not sure which."

"I beg your pardon?"

"Just...ask later, okay?"

Roger didn't look particularly keen on the idea of not knowing what happened to his car until later, but he let it go.

"So, if you're sworn to secrecy, what's next?"

"We keep investigating. I'm not going to be able to sleep for the next few months anyway, so I'm heading over to the Ashcraft place to see what I can find out."

Chapter Twelve

I left my car alongside the road about six blocks from Michael and Jennifer's house. I was getting tired of all this walking around, but I wanted to cut down on the chances that I'd get busted for burglary. About three blocks from their house it suddenly occurred to me that my pockets were missing something vitally important, such as my car keys. After uttering one of the ruder phrases I'd spoken in my life, I jogged back to where I'd parked my automobile.

It was gone.

I used the word "shit" numerous times.

Then I realized that this wasn't even where I'd left it—I was still a block away. It was pretty clear that my mind was no longer the well-oiled, smooth-running piece of machinery it had been a little over a day ago.

I jogged over to the place where I'd left my car, and was actually surprised to find it there, fully intact. The keys were still in the ignition, and the doors were locked. I suppose I could've called a locksmith, but I didn't want to stand around waiting so I picked up a nice-sized rock and smashed open the passenger-side window, spraying safety glass all over the place. I leaned inside, retrieved my keys, and headed back to Michael's house.

Nobody was out for a late-night stroll and I didn't see anyone with their faces pressed against the neighboring windows, so I figured it was safe enough to hurry into the back-yard. Once there, I saw that there was a door that probably led to the garage, and a couple of large windows in the main part of the house.

I reached for the doorknob, mentally reviewing my plan of action should an alarm go off:

Stand in dumbfounded shock for exactly two seconds.
Run away very fast.

I tested the doorknob. Locked. I tested it again, in case some higher power had fixed the situation for me, but no luck. I'd left my lock-picking tools in a previous life, so my only choice now was a window.

I peeked through one of the windows, a sliding one which was up about five feet from the ground. Through it, I could see the kitchen. Hopefully they had beer in the fridge, be-cause I was gonna need a good drink after this. I pressed my hands against the glass and tried to raise it, but the window was, of course, locked.

I hadn't even realized that I was still holding the rock I'd used to break my car window. So, I'd have to test how heavily the neighbors slept.

I raised the rock to the glass and gave it a couple prelimi-nary taps, as if the window might be kind enough to shatter quietly. I listened for a possible meteorite or exploding ve-hicle that might cover the noise, but none were handy.

I took a deep breath, and then hurled the rock through the glass, near the bottom. I was confident that if Michael's corpse had been buried in the backyard at that moment, the crash would have awakened him, but at least no alarm went off. I stood silently for a full minute, watching for lights turn-ing on in the neighboring homes and listening for voices say-ing "Thelma, go fetch my shotgun!" but it didn't appear that my ruckus had disturbed anyone.

I reached through the hole and unlocked the window, then carefully raised it. I gripped the frame with both hands and pulled myself inside, knocking over a stack of dishes that had been resting on the counter. They fell to the lino-leum floor and shattered with a sound that reminded me of policemen firing gunshots at suspected burglars, though I may have just been a tad edgy.

I hopped off the counter and took a moment to admire

the kitchen. Neatly decorated, if a bit antiseptic for my tastes. I opened the refrigerator and found nothing to drink but bottled water, so I proceeded into the living room.

Nothing especially interesting in here, either, except for a couple of pieces of art that were so tacky I'm surprised the wall didn't come to life and fling them away. I think one of them was supposed to be a chicken, but it also might have been a portrait of Albert Einstein. A black cat, sleeping on the floor, looked up at me and meowed as if to say "Please remove your unworthy hide from my palace."

I walked down a hallway, which was decorated with framed photographs of Michael, Jennifer, and other people who I presume were relatives. There was a picture of Michael and Jennifer at their wedding, the happy couple shoving cake into each other's faces (an idea Helen had nixed well before our own ceremony).

The first doorway led to a bathroom. Frilly shower curtain, exotic soaps that I'm sure nobody was ever allowed to use, blue water in the toilet...high-class stuff.

The next doorway led to an office, which had been ransacked big-time. There were books and papers all over the floor, as well as a bunch of torn horror movie posters. The corners of some of the posters could be seen still taped to the wall. A desk had been overturned, and a chair ripped apart, with cushion stuffing scattered everywhere. All the drawers of a filing cabinet were open and the contents had been dumped on the floor in front of it. There was some computer equipment that looked like it had been smashed apart with a baseball bat.

I crouched down and began to sift through the papers, hoping to find something like a signed confession or coffin schematics. What I found were lots of papers with cryptic budget figures (I somehow skipped accounting as one of my majors), uninteresting bills, junk mail, warranties for major appliances, and other stuff that seemed to have no relevance to a man being buried alive.

I searched through the office for about ten minutes, and found nothing that seemed even remotely helpful. I wondered if the person who'd made the mess had ended up with the same result. It was going to take hours to go through everything piece-by-piece, and I decided I'd better at least check out the rest of the house before I resigned myself to that task.

When I turned on the light in the bedroom, it was imme-diately obvious what the search had been all about.

A large picture of Jennifer rested on the bed, the plastic frame cracked. A nail on the wall showed exactly where it had previously been hanging...covering your standard-issue wall safe. The door to the safe was ajar, and rather than be-ing a combination dial it had been opened with a key.

Perhaps a key smelling of Michael Ashcraft's foot odor.

I walked around the bed and swung the safe door open all the way. Empty. That wasn't much of a surprise, since the killer probably hadn't been dumb enough to go through all this work and then forget the booty. *I* might have been dumb enough to do something like that, but not the killer.

A closer examination of the inside of the safe revealed a small hole in the back. I wasn't sticking my finger in that thing, so I returned to the office for a pencil. That done, I slowly inserted the pencil into the hole, encountering a bit of resistance right away. There was some sort of spring inside.

The significance of a spring-loaded hole inside a safe then became extremely clear to me, and I thanked whatever deity was handy that the booby trap hadn't been reloaded before I got here.

I returned the door of the safe to its original position, and then began to look around the area. A few seconds later I heard the front door open.

I hadn't even heard a car approach, which didn't mean much if the intruder had parked elsewhere like I had. I quickly moved around the bed on my tiptoes as the intruder shut the door behind him. I could either hide under the bed or in the closet. I picked the closet.

I opened the closet door and threw up my hands to de-fend myself against the pile of pillows and blankets that came crashing down upon me. The closet was absolutely packed. I had chosen poorly.

Before I could rethink my hiding place, I turned toward the doorway and saw The Apparition. I didn't much like see-ing him again, but I liked seeing the gun he was pointing at me even less.

"Hands in the air."

I did as he said.

"Turn around."

I turned around. The Apparition stepped over to me and pressed the barrel of his revolver against the back of my neck.

"Walk to the living room."

I walked at a slow, steady pace, trying not to do anything, such as tumble forward, that might panic him and cause a large hole to be added to my neck. Once we were in the living room, he gave me a violent shove and I collapsed onto the sofa.

The Apparition remained in the center of the room. He scratched at his beard with the handle of the revolver then pointed the barrel at me. "Do you know what time it is?" he asked, irritably.

I shook my head.

"It's practically *dawn*, that's what time it is! What is it with you bein' out all night? How the hell am I supposed to get any sleep? I'm not as young as I used to be. I don't do well when I'm forced to prance all over town cleanin' up after people! Give it a fuckin' rest!"

"I'm a bit confused," I admitted. "Are you the killer I'm looking for?"

"No, I am not the killer. I work for the killer. I work long, ridiculously late hours for the killer because you won't go to goddamn bed! Do you know where I was when you tripped the silent alarm? I was asleep, dreamin' that I was in a hot tub with a half dozen Victoria's Secret models! Do you know how hard it is for me to get that dream? Do you?"

I shook my head.

"It's hard as hell!"

"I'm sorry."

The Apparition began to pace back and forth. "I mean, it's bad enough that I'm reburyin' coffins that you're too lazy to cover and getting' rid of cars with little pieces of people inside, but I should at least be able to get a tiny bit of sleep before I'm out here checkin' on you again! I know my boss is encouraging you to investigate, but why not stick to normal workin' hours, huh? Let me get some rest. How does that sound?"

"Who is your boss?" I asked.

"Oh, golly, you almost got me there!" said The Apparition, sarcastically. "With a cunning question like that I almost blew the whole thing! You're so damn clever I don't know why you haven't figured it all out already!"

"Hey, it was worth a shot," I said. "You can never underestimate how foolish people can be in stressful situations."

"Yeah, yeah, whatever. You know, I think I should just shoot you." He pointed the revolver at my face and took two steps forward. "Blow your head off then get myself some sleep."

"You're not really going to blow anybody's head off with that thing," I noted. "Even Dirty Harry exaggerated, and his gun was bigger than yours."

The Apparition glared at me. "Don't push me. I'm tired and cranky."

"Won't your boss be upset if you kill me?"

"My boss is welcome to pucker up and kiss my hemorrhoid-ridden butt."

"That's a poor work ethic."

"Be quiet. Anyway, if I were put in physical danger I'd be justified in shootin' you, and who's going to know if I shot you while you were sittin' peacefully on the couch or if you were lungin' at me with a crowbar?"

"Well, if my blood was all over the couch that might provide a pretty decent clue," I pointed out.

"It doesn't really matter either way. If I don't kill you, things proceed as planned. If I do kill you, your part transfers to your buddy Roger. No big deal."

"I don't know, Roger's pretty unmotivated."

"Then I kill him and it transfers to your wife. Still no big deal."

My insides tightened a bit at that. "I'm the one who messed around in the graveyard and played Find the Spare Change in the Head. I think I've got some investment in this thing."

The Apparition nodded and lowered the gun. "You've got a point there. Maybe I won't kill you after all."

"Well, thank you. You're a kind and generous soul."

Then he shrugged and pointed the gun at my face again. "But to be honest, I'm already sick of you. I hope you can make peace with yourself in the next second and a half, because that's all you've got to live."

CHAPTER THIRTEEN

Okay, obviously I didn't die or I wouldn't be able to relate this tender little narrative. Unless, of course, I'm a ghost, writing these words through an Ouija board. That *would* be pretty cool, but also incredibly time consuming, and the human I was channeling through would probably try to steal all the credit. Plus, becoming a ghost at the hands of a man named The Apparition would just be too ironic. So I lived.

"I know where the money is," I blurted out somewhere around the half-second mark.

The Apparition hesitated. "What money?"

"The money your boss was looking for."

"What are you babblin' about?"

"Here, let me speak in a way that you might understand." I spoke slowly, enunciating each word, as if talking to a not-very-bright infant. "*I know where the money is.* And if your boss wants it, you'd be well advised not to shoot me before I tell you where it is."

"My boss isn't lookin' for any money. You're bluffin' to save your life."

"No, I'm not. Did you notice the ceiling?"

The Apparition glanced up for a second. "What about the ceiling?"

"It's the clue that answered the riddle. A neat little puzzle, actually. Your boss would appreciate it. Looks like Michael

Ashcraft came up with some interesting stuff on his own. I didn't figure it out until right before you showed up, but it's pretty clever."

The Apparition looked up once more, and then quickly returned his attention to me. "There's nothin' on the ceiling."

"Sure there is. Look at the watermark."

"I don't see any watermark."

"Well, now, that's the trick. You've got to look at it from the right angle. I'll show you, but you have to promise not to kill me."

"I'm not promising you anything 'cept that I'm gonna shoot you the second this starts to bore me. And I'm gettin' very close."

"Okay, fine, just back up a couple steps."

Keeping the revolver focused on me, The Apparition took two steps backwards. "There's nothin' there."

"Look carefully at the way the light hits the whitewash. When you're in exactly the right place, you'll see what I'm talking about."

"I don't see anything."

"Well, gee, Mr. The Apparition, you must not be in exactly the right place, then. Would you like me to get up and show you?"

"You keep your butt planted to that couch or you're gettin' a bullet through the eye."

"Sounds good. Try one step to the left."

The Apparition took a step to the left, his foot coming down exactly where I'd hoped it would—on the tail of the cat. The cat let out a screech and latched onto his leg, claws and fangs moving like a garbage disposal. In the second that The Apparition was distracted, I lunged out of my seat and dove at him, my hands colliding with his throat and knocking him to the floor. I crouched down and smashed my knuckles into his wrist and made a grinding motion until he released his grip on the revolver, then I snatched it up and pushed it against his nose.

"Please get this cat off me," he said.

"The cat stays," I informed him. "Who do you work for?"

"None of your business."

"Unless you'd like a demonstration of the world's best cure for nasal decongestion, you'll start talking."

"If you kill me, I won't be able to say a word."

"Then I'll shoot you somewhere that won't kill you."

"Then somebody'll hear the shots and call the police."

"Then you'll go to jail."

"I'd say that you shot me when I was tryin' to stop you from burglarizin' my friend's house. Could you please get this cat off me?"

I could see that getting any information from him was going to require extreme measures. I stood up, keeping the revolver pointed at him, and gently nudged the cat off his leg with my foot. It took off running down the hall, probably unaware that it had saved my life. Maybe I'd name it Reverse Snowflake.

"C'mon, Mr. App, it's time to start spilling your guts," I said. "After seeing that tape, you'd better believe that I'm going to do whatever it takes to get you to talk."

"Well then you should get started."

"I will."

The Apparition grinned. "Feelin' kind of tough right now, aren't you? I bet you don't get many chances to beat up a sleep-deprived old man."

"This is your last chance to answer some questions peacefully," I warned him. "There's a whole kitchen filled with utensils that will make the process much less pleasant."

"Hmmmm...let me see if you're scaring me yet." The Apparition pretended to think that over. "Nope, not yet. I'll let you know if things change."

"Fine," I said, motioning toward the recliner with the gun. "Why don't you have a seat?"

"Nah, I'm pretty comfortable here on the floor."

"I said, why don't you have a seat?"

"And I said I'm pretty comfortable here on the floor."

"Do you honestly think that after watching a guy being tortured to death with a spork I'm going to hesitate in shooting a sicko like you?"

The Apparition nodded. "Yeah, I do."

I hate confident people.

"Listen to me, you piece of shit," I said, hoping that profanity would indicate exactly how serious I was. "If you don't get up right now and park your ass on that couch, I'm going to push this gun against your kneecap, pull the trigger, and

hope that our neighbors are heavy sleepers. Do you understand?"

"I understand, but I still ain't getting' up."

This wasn't fair. I had the gun, so I was supposed to have
the upper hand.

"I'm not kidding," I said.

"I never said you were."

Damn, damn, damn! Now I either had to make good on
my threat or be seen as a nothing-but-talk weenie. And I
didn't think I could work up the nerve to actually blow a hole
through his knee.

Okay, if intimidation wasn't going to work at the moment,
I'd just have to rely on good old fashioned brute force. I walked
over, grabbed The Apparition by his shirt collar, and yanked
him to his feet. Then I clamped my hand on the back of his
neck and forced him into the dining room, where I slammed
him down onto a chair.

"Stay there," I said.

I walked into the kitchen, keeping the revolver pointed at
him at all times. He didn't move, so he obviously had *some*
doubts about my unwillingness to shoot. I searched through
some drawers until I found what I was looking for. Duct tape.

"Sure you don't want to talk?" I asked, twirling the spool
of tape around my index finger. "You're about to become a lot
less comfortable."

"You know, I'm *tryin'* to get scared, but for some reason I
just can't. I dunno what it is."

Fine. The cheeky bastard was getting taped to the chair.
I set the gun on the counter and prepared myself in case he
should make any sudden moves. I punched him in the stomach to keep him from squirming, then wrapped the tape
around each of his hands, fixing them to the arms of the
chair. Once that was done, I wrapped the tape around his
chest until the spool was empty.

"Comfy?" I asked.

He didn't respond. I went back to the drawers and picked
up a meat cleaver. I wished I could do some fancy moves,
tossing it in the air like a master chef, but I figured that accidentally chopping off my own hand would cost me some intimidation points.

"Okay, we're going to play a little game," I said. "It's called

Tell Me What I Want To Know Or I'll Cut Off Your Fingers One By One You Psychotic Bastard."

"I'm not a psycho, I only work for one," The Apparition corrected.

"You're not taking this very seriously. Don't you like your fingers? Haven't they provided you with many years of service? Think about all the times you've had the convenience of being able to hold objects or wear rings. If you don't cooperate now you'll never be able to flip the bird at a lousy driver ever again."

"I'll have to deal with it."

Why did he have to be so difficult? If I had to resort to genuine torture to get the information out of him, well, I'd do it! To save five innocent people I could certainly bring myself to sadistically torture one scumbag.

"Okay," I said. I pressed the blade of the meat cleaver against his little finger. "Say goodbye to Mr. Pinky."

"There's gonna be a lot of blood," he said.

"I've seen blood."

"Then don't let me stop you."

I applied a little more pressure to the cleaver, not enough to even break the skin, let alone chop through the bone. My stomach was beginning to churn, but I had to be strong. One finger gone and this jerk would tell me anything I wanted to know. I balled my other hand into a fist and raised it above the cleaver, preparing to slam it down.

"Last chance," I said.

"I consider myself fully warned."

I brought my fist down. But right before striking the cleaver I quickly changed direction and slammed my hand over my mouth. I darted over to the counter and promptly vomited in the sink. It was not a grand moment for my dignity.

The Apparition began to laugh loudly.

I wiped my mouth off on my sleeve and gave him the most evil look of which I was capable. It would probably have been more evil if I hadn't been positively sick to my stomach. I can pretty much handle snuff videos and people ripping their eyes out, but being the instigator of gruesome violence myself was way too much.

"Nice show, Mayhem," The Apparition sneered. "Glad to

see I didn't misjudge you! Maybe for an encore you can piss your pants!"

I coughed a few times, and then turned on the faucet to rinse away the evidence of my inability to handle the rough stuff. I retrieved the meat cleaver from where it had fallen on the floor and placed it back against his finger. "Let's try this again," I said, my voice squeaking in a most unmasculine manner.

"Oh, give it up," The Apparition suggested. "What do you care if those people die, anyway? Face it, you ain't got what it takes to stop this. You're a loser."

"You think I'm a loser?" I asked, raising the meat cleaver. "Is that what you think? We'll see who's a loser after I slam this cleaver right through your skull!" I began to pace back and forth, swinging the cleaver wildly through the air. "I've had it with your bullshit! I've had it! You don't want to talk, that's fine! I don't care anymore! I'm done being your boss's freakin' puppet!"

I kicked one of the chairs as hard as I could, knocking it over. "You think I'm a loser, my parents think I'm a loser, my wife thinks I'm a loser, fine! You hear me? Fine!" I slammed the cleaver into the table, imbedding it in the wood. I started to pry it out, but it was stuck pretty firmly and I didn't want The Apparition to see me struggle with it. Instead I pulled open the top drawer with so much force that it popped all the way out, scattering utensils all over the floor with a huge crash. I reached down, but grabbed a piece of a broken plate rather than a fork or knife.

"I've had it!" I nearly shouted. "I'm ending this whole thing right here, right now, starting with you!" I raised the broken plate like a dagger, and then smashed it against the side of the chair so that splinters of glass sprayed up onto his face. Then I pushed the tip of the remaining chunk against his throat, hard enough that a small trickle of blood ran down his neck.

The Apparition had gone completely pale. Apparently he'd decided that I was starting to become a threat to his personal safety.

He stiffened, made a soft gasping sound, and then slumped forward, motionless.

"Uh..." I said.

I reached over and pressed my fingers against his neck. No pulse. It looked as if I'd given the old guy a fatal heart attack. I was getting a little tired of watching these.

I stood there in shock for a long, long moment. Then I reacted.

"You son of a bitch!" I shouted at him. "You miserable prick! Where do you get off dying on me?" I resisted the urge to kick his chair over and settled for kicking the refrigerator instead. That hurt, so I quit.

I returned to the living room and plopped down on the recliner. Great. Just great. Wonderful. Super. Dandy. Delightful. Peachy.

Shit!

Reverse Snowflake walked into the room and hissed at me. I told him to shut up and go away.

Okay, technically I wasn't much worse off than I had been before I'd broken into the house, except that I was directly responsible for a dead body in the kitchen, and when the police eventually became involved I was going to have a bit of difficulty explaining it. The self-defense argument doesn't quite hold water when the victim is tied to a chair with duct tape.

I wondered how the killer would react to the news.

And then I brightened. Since The Apparition probably hadn't expected to spend the rest of his evening dead, maybe he hadn't gone to the trouble of covering his tracks. His truck was outside, and maybe he was even carrying a wallet. There might be a clue yet!

* * *

The Apparition was not carrying a wallet, and a thorough search of his truck provided nothing of interest...with the exception of a little black book containing the killer's phone number.

CHAPTER FOURTEEN

It was lying there right on the seat. I quickly flipped through the book and concluded that The Apparition didn't have much of a social life—most of the pages were blank. There were listings for eight different pizza places, as well as addresses and phone numbers for Michael Ashcraft, Dominick Griffin, Linda Hanson, Rachel Mallory, Farley Soukup, and Carl Underall.

There was also one number, written on the bottom of the "A" page, without any description. I went back inside Michael's house and called it.

After three rings, somebody picked up, but didn't speak.

"Hello?" I said.

Silence.

"Is anybody there?"

A click, then a dial tone. Okay, it *was* kind of inconsiderate to be calling at this time of the night/morning. I would've hung up, too.

Less than a minute later, while I stood around trying to decide what to do with The Apparition, Michael's phone rang. I picked up the receiver and said nothing.

"Hello, Andrew," said the computer-generated monotone.

"Hi, Chuckles. How's it hangin'?"

"How did you get the phone number you just called?"

"It was the weirdest thing. I was trying to call Oswald Hankensnorker's Psychic Connection when my fingers slipped and I got you. Small world, huh?"

"Where's The Apparition?"

"He's safe, for now. But if you want to ever see his cute little beard again, I think we need to talk."

"We are talking."

"And I appreciate it. So, what do you think of a trade? I give you your buddy, you give me the prisoners?"

"He's not my buddy."

"Okay, then I'll give you your faithful employee, how about that?"

"Let me speak to him."

"No can do," I said. "He's kind of unconscious at the moment."

"What makes you think I care what happens to him? Go ahead and kill him."

"I didn't say I was going to kill him. But I'll bet you anything that once I start turning his life into an episode of *Ghoulish Delights* he'll lead me right to your place. Why not save us the mess?"

"You overestimate how much he knows."

"I bet he knows enough."

"Then get it out of him. Do you have any spiders handy? He hates spiders. Put a tarantula down the back of his shirt and he'll tell you anything."

"Well, thank you so much for the helpful hint. If I should happen to find a tarantula lying around I'll be sure to try it."

"It's almost time for me to hang up," said the voice. "When you start torturing The Apparition, tell him I said hi. You're doing fine work, Mayhem. Keep it up."

"Look, I've just about had it with your crap."

"Too bad. I have more crap to give you."

"Well, I'm getting pretty close to the quitting point. I want to know what the hell I have to do to make you let those people go."

"The same thing you've been doing, except that there's a new rule now. Don't visit any of our homes. You do, the prisoners die. By the way, I wouldn't want you to waste your valuable time, so I'll say right now that the phone number you called goes to the same cellular phone you used earlier. It's under Jennifer's name."

He was one heck of a fast typist. "Well, you're just filled

with helpful tidbits tonight, aren't you?"

"Here's one more. You'll get another tape tomorrow. If you thought the last one was bad, this one will have your brain leaking out of your ears. Good night."

The killer hung up. I redialed the number and let it ring about twenty times before giving up.

* * *

After some thought, I took the lazy route and decided to leave Michael's house the way it was. The Apparition could just sit there taped to the chair being dead. I was eventually going to have to tell the whole story anyway, so there was no sense in covering my tracks, and it's not like he was a fine, upstanding member of the community who deserved the best care upon his untimely passing. Let him stink up the place.

I couldn't get Reverse Snowflake to come out from under Michael's bed, so I made sure he had plenty of food and water. I couldn't adopt him, for fear that he might shred my children, but I decided I'd make sure he found a good home after this whole thing blew over.

I left The Apparition's truck in the driveway and walked back to my own car. It was still there, so I drove back to Roger's place, borrowed a blanket and an alarm clock, and stretched out on the floor to get a couple hours of sleep.

* * *

The alarm went off at the unholy hour of five-fifteen. I got up off the couch, staggered around for a moment wondering what planet I was currently residing on, then used Roger's shower. The soap didn't jolt me into a state of euphoric alertness like the commercials said it would, but I felt a bit more human.

During my shower, I came up with a plan. Not necessarily a good plan. Possibly a very bad plan. Definitely a risky plan. Sort of a pray-your-instincts-are-right-because-otherwise-you're-100%-screwed plan. But a plan nevertheless.

I woke Roger up by dropping a few cubes of ice on his chest. Once in college when he'd been extremely hung-over I'd used an entire cooler's worth to wake him up, but now that we were mature adults a few cubes were sufficient. Theresa and Kyle weren't any more keen to get up than Roger had been, but I eventually got them dressed and into my car. The kids were too sleepy to even engage in much combat on the way to the gym, but once we pulled into the parking lot they both perked up.

"Ooh! Ooh! Can I play on the treadmill if they have one?" asked Theresa.

"Probably not," I told her. "I need both of you to behave and not get in anyone's way. These people aren't here to have fun, they're here to get in shape."

"I'm in shape," said Kyle, flexing what existed of a muscle.

"You sure are, Hulk. Now if you behave yourselves, we'll have pizza for lunch."

Is the frequent use of bribery to control behavior the sign of a bad parent? As soon as the killer was apprehended, I was going to have to work on that.

I'd explained to Roger that his job was to sit in the car and watch for anything remotely suspicious, particularly if it took the form of any Ghoulish Delights employees. He had no problem with that, probably because it didn't involve hanging around a graveyard for a few hours.

We went inside. "Are you a member?" asked the man behind the front desk. He had biceps that looked like a bowling ball had been surgically implanted in each arm, and gave me a look that showed he considered himself very, very strong while he considered me very, very weak.

"No, but I'm here to see Rachel Mallory."

"You should consider the benefits of membership. A strong, healthy body goes a long way toward protecting one's children."

"Wow!" exclaimed Kyle, dragging his attention away from the pictures hanging on the wall long enough to notice the man. "Are you Hercules?" The man favored him with a nod. "Yes I am." To me, he said, "Membership is only thirty dollars a month, and carries with it the benefit that young children mistake you for Hercules. What do you say?"

"We'll see how things go with Rachel," I said. I noticed that Theresa was looking a bit starry-eyed, so I waved my hand in front of her face to being her back to reality.

"Hey, Rachel!" the man called out. "Some guy is here to see you!"

Rachel walked into the lobby, wearing a blue spandex uniform that really showed off her athletic physique. "Wow!" exclaimed Kyle. "Are you Xena, Warrior Princess?"

"No, I'm Wonder Woman," Rachel told him. "Shall we start your workout?"

"Sure, that sounds great," I said, only so Hercules wouldn't mock me. We followed her back to the weight room. Only a couple of people were using it, a woman in incredible physical shape and a man who really needed to lift a few more weights before he'd be in good enough shape to attract the woman.

"I guess we'll start off with some stretches," said Rachel, leading us to a floor mat. "Everyone take off your shoes."

"This really wasn't supposed to be an exercise session. I just wanted to ask you a few questions about Michael."

"You can ask me questions while we get in a good workout. You need one. Get those shoes off."

Theresa and Kyle excitedly removed their footwear, and Theresa launched into some jumping jacks. I considered mentioning that I wasn't dressed for a workout, but then made the astute observation that she wouldn't care.

"Now, I want everyone to touch your right toe with your left hand." Rachel reached down and touched her right toe with her left hand, as if it were no problem whatsoever. I reached down and did the same thing.

"Don't bend your knees," Rachel said.

I tried to touch my toe without bending my knees and was not entirely successful. But I did better than Kyle, who tumbled forward and hit his face on the mat.

"He's missing a few motor skills," I explained.

"Must take after his father."

I reached down and touched my toe just to spite her. I refused to say anything about the sharp pain in my back.

"Now touch your left toe with your right hand, and alternate to the count of twenty. Andrew, you can ask your questions now."

"When did you last see Michael?"

"Two...three...last Thursday, right before he left for Europe...six...seven..."

"Was he acting unusual?"

"...eight...nine...no, not unusual in a bad way... twelve...thirteen...he was really excited about his trip... sixteen...seventeen...couldn't stop talking about it...twenty."

"So he seemed genuinely excited?"

"Sure. Wouldn't you be?" Rachel smiled at Theresa and Kyle. "Do you kids want to show me who can do the most push-ups?"

"Me!" shouted Theresa.

"Prove it!"

My children dropped to the floor and began doing push-ups.

Rachel grinned as she watched them go at it. Whoever the killer might be, I was sure it wasn't her. Not that any of the others seemed like killers, either, but for some unexplainable reason I just had a gut feeling that Rachel was innocent. Which was good, because this was a crucial element in my plan. If I was going to make any progress in finding the killer, I had to take this huge risk.

"So what's up with the questions about Mike? You sound like a cop, not a journalist."

"I'm not a journalist," I said. I motioned her to follow me to another part of the room, where my children couldn't hear us. "I take it Carl or Farley didn't get in touch with you last night?"

"No, I kept the phone off the hook. I don't like being bothered when I'm reading. So are you a cop?"

"No."

"A detective?"

"Rachel, I need to tell you something very important, but I need your promise that you won't share it with anyone, no matter what."

"I'd like to make that promise, but anyone puts some red-hot spikes under my toenails and I'm blabbing."

Since that wasn't entirely out of the realm of possibility, I let it go. "It's about somebody in Ghoulish Delights. At least I'm pretty sure it is. And I don't know who else I can trust."

"You don't know who else you can trust? Look, Andy, if you're trying out for an acting role in our movies, at least get some better dialogue first."

"This isn't an audition. And don't call me Andy."

"Sorry."

"Would you like some more clichéd dialogue? How about this: Innocent lives depend on you helping me. And innocent lives are at risk if you repeat any of what I'm about to tell you."

"Whose lives?" Rachel asked.

"I don't know their names. Five people locked away some-where, kidnapped by someone you work with."

Rachel stared at me for a moment, then looked over at Theresa and Kyle. "Hey, there are jump ropes in the corner if you want!"

"Hooray!" shouted Theresa, as she raced her brother to the corner and won.

"All right, Andrew, you've got me interested enough to give my promise. What's the story?"

"Michael and Jennifer Ashcraft are dead. Michael was buried alive, and Jennifer was stabbed to death then chopped into pieces that were hidden in my best friend's automobile."

"*What*?" asked Rachel with disbelief.

"I'm sorry, I should have eased into that. But I'm com-pletely serious. They're dead, and the killer has me involved in some kind of sick game."

"What do you mean, some kind of sick game?"

I described my adventures in complete gory detail. The color drained from her face as I spoke, and by the time I'd finished she looked positively ill. "I'm sorry, I need a drink of water," she said. "I'll be right back."

I didn't really want to let her out of my sight, but it wasn't like I could prevent her from going anywhere. I desperately hoped that telling her had been the right thing to do, but to find out what was going on I absolutely had to get some sort of inside information. She left the weight room, and I went over to make sure my kids were playing nicely.

Rachel returned a couple of minutes later, not looking much better. She sat down on one of the weight machines, and I joined her.

"So you're sure it's someone at Ghoulish Delights?" she asked.

"Pretty sure."

"Any idea who?"

I shook my head. "That's why I need you. Do you know them all pretty well?"

"Sure. I mean, I don't consider them a second family or anything, but we know each other fairly well. At least I thought we did. I certainly didn't think any of them could be a mur-derer, especially not as sadistic as the way you described."

"We need to be careful, because I don't know what kind of resources the killer has," I said. "I'm sure he hasn't had a chance to put a bug on me or anything since my last complete change of clothes, but there's a good chance that more people are helping him, and they could be watching."

"You think it's a he?"

"No, it's just too hard to carry on a conversation and worry about being gender neutral. Anyway, that would only eliminate Linda."

"Or me."

"Well, I sort of already eliminated you, thus this whole conversation."

"And why is that?"

I shrugged. "I'm hoping it's because I possess a remarkable sense of character, and not that I'm a complete idiot."

"So what do you want to ask me?"

"For starters, who in Ghoulish Delights was closest to Jennifer, personally? I'm thinking maybe a lover."

"Jeez, I don't think I can help you with that one, either. I've never noticed that any of us were all that close to her. I wouldn't put it past her to have cheated on Mike, but I can't imagine it being with anyone at work. Dominick, maybe, but he and Linda are pretty serious. I don't think Carl's even kissed a girl yet, and who could be attracted to Farley?"

"No one in any universe I've ever inhabited," I admitted. "Do they all own computers?"

"I don't know. Carl and Farley definitely do. I think Linda does, but I can't say for sure. I'm sorry, I'm not being much help, am I?"

"Sure you are. Another question...does anyone in the group own a bow and arrow? Maybe a crossbow?"

"Yeah, Dominick does. He has an amazing collection of weaponry from what I hear, all kinds of stuff. But he also has a bunch of stuff that he leaves in the office, that anyone could have taken."

The Mad Archer hadn't really demonstrated any out-of-the-ordinary skill, so this knowledge didn't help much. "The guy I sort of scared to death last night, The Apparition, do you know him? Your name was in his address book."

"I don't know anyone socially by the name of The Apparition, but describe him."

"Old guy. Big white beard. Sort of a weird facial bone structure, a little off-center."

"That's Jake!" Rachel exclaimed. "We hired him right when we started Ghoulish Delights, but Mike fired him. I don't think he even lasted a week. I'd forgotten all about him. You say he had my address?"

I nodded. "Everyone else's, too. I need to know, have you ever gotten the impression that Ghoulish Delights is more than the part that you're familiar with? Because I think it's a cover for something a lot more profitable, and a lot more demented."

"The snuff video, right? I know I sound like I have no observational powers whatsoever, but if the Ghoulish Delights I know is a cover for a snuff film operation, I had absolutely no idea. How many tapes did you say there were?"

"I didn't. I've got the one I found in the coffin, and the killer said he'd give me another one today. But from Jennifer's introduction it sounded like part of a series. You've got the real-life murder part, and the fancy introduction...it's either a nice little treat for some depraved clients, or just a creepy way that Michael and Jennifer entertained themselves."

"If he even knew about it. So far you only have proof that Jennifer was involved."

"You're right. And him finding out about it could have been what started this whole—"

I stopped talking as I saw Roger crutch his way into the weight room. "Hey, our story is paying us a visit," he announced, as he was followed by Dominick and Linda. Neither of them appeared happy; Dominick furious, Linda distraught.

I glanced quickly at Rachel, who was looking a bit panicky. I hoped to God she wouldn't blow the whole deal.

CHAPTER FIFTEEN

"Do you mind telling me who you really are?" Dominick demanded, taking long, purposeful strides toward me.

"You must've talked to Carl or Farley," I said, keeping my cool.

"You're damn right. Farley called me last night. You've got a lot of nerve pretending to be a reporter when you're just some pathetic excuse for a detective. Mike was a good friend of mine, and I can't believe you didn't tell us something happened to him!"

"It's for his own good," I said.

"Oh, yeah, I'm sure. How exactly does that work?"

"There's a lot more to the situation that Jennifer doesn't want me to discuss. I'm sorry, but she's my client and I have to respect her wishes."

"Where is she now?"

"That's confidential."

"Screw confidential! I want to know what's going on!"

Dominick raised a fist as if to hit me. Linda put her hand on his shoulder to calm him, while Rachel stepped between us. "Settle down," she said.

"I don't want to settle down!"

"Settle down or I'll do it for you."

"You're sticking up for him?" asked Dominick, incredulous. "He lied to everyone! He should've been out there trying to find Mike instead of wasting our time with this *Dearly Demented* bullshit!"

"Tell me, Dominick," said Rachel, "are you currently a licensed private investigator?"

"What? No."

"Well, our friend Andrew here is. Which means he knows what he's doing."

Less true words were never spoken, but I certainly didn't jump in and correct her.

"So, if we want to increase our chances of ever seeing Mike again, we're going to have to trust him. Does that make sense to you?"

Dominick still looked like he wanted to squish my head between a pair of barbells, but he gave the faintest of nods and stepped back. Linda breathed a sigh of relief and took him by the hand.

"What's your next step?" asked Dominick.

"I'm currently following up on several leads," I said.

"Like what?"

"They're confidential."

"Don't give me that! I want to know what you're doing to find my friend. What are the police doing?"

"They're looking into it," I said. "But Jennifer wants this all kept as quiet as possible."

"Why?"

"She just does."

"That doesn't make any sense! Unless she was involved in his disappearance, why would she want it kept quiet? Does she think there's going to be a scandal or something? I'm sorry, but I'm really confused here."

"Sweetie, relax," said Linda, patting his elbow with her free hand. "They're doing what they can."

"I'm not sure I believe that."

Rachel spoke up. "Dominick, I know you're upset. We all are. But I have every confidence that Andrew is doing everything possible to bring Mike back to us." Her voice cracked on the last few words.

I felt like a total cretin for standing here trying to boost Dominick and Linda's hopes when I knew full well that Michael wasn't coming back, but what choice did I have?

"I promise I'll let you know as soon as I find out something," I assured him.

"You said you already have a few leads. That's considered finding out something. Why not share those?" asked Dominick.

"Okay, that's enough," said Rachel. "Linda, could you please take your boyfriend home and find a way to relax him?"

"C'mon, sweetie, let's go." Linda started to lead Dominick toward the doorway. "If there's anything we can do to help, please call us. Are we still on for the taping today?"

Rachel glanced at me, and I gave her a light nod. "Yeah," she said. "I'll call Carl and Farley to make sure they know it hasn't been cancelled."

"Okay, see you then." Linda and Dominick left.

"So when do we tell them?" asked Rachel.

"I don't know," I admitted. "I don't know what the killer has planned besides giving me a second tape. He said something about it being too late for him, about not being around soon. Do any of the Ghoulish Delights people have medical problems that you know about?"

"Carl has asthma, but nothing serious. Certainly nothing terminal, at least not that they've said anything about. Have you checked hospital records?"

"That was on the agenda for today. My wife's a nurse, so I was hoping she'd be able to assist with that. Not that she can do much while stuck in bed with a broken leg, but I don't exactly have a long list of connections."

Rachel thought for a long moment. "I want to help you in any way I can, but I really don't know what else to tell you. Is there anything you want me to do?"

I shook my head. "Nothing. Don't go around asking questions or anything like that...I don't want to tip off the killer that I told you. If it's all right, I'm still coming to the taping today. Having everyone together in one place may be helpful, especially if the killer doesn't think you know what's going on. You might catch something that Roger and I miss."

"Sounds good." She wiped a tear from her eye. "Sorry, I'm still in shock. By the way, I meant to say this earlier, but if this is a prank, I will personally break every single bone in your body."

"I wish this was a joke, believe me," I said. "I'm going to head off now, because quite honestly if I don't get a bit more sleep the killer could juggle chainsaws at the taping and I wouldn't notice."

"All right." She gave me the address and wished me luck. I gathered my offspring and we walked out of the weight room and past the front desk.

"So, you becoming a member?" asked Hercules.

I couldn't come up with a single even remotely smart-ass thing to say, so I merely shook my head. This was bad. I really needed sleep.

And as we walked outside and saw the package resting on the hood of my car, I realized that I wasn't going to be getting any rest in the near future.

"Someone left us a present!" Kyle exclaimed. He started to rush forward toward the colorfully-wrapped gift, which was about the size of a milk crate, but I quickly scooped him up by the waist and held him back.

"It's not a kid present, it's a grown-up present," I said, dangling him upside-down to the accompaniment of a severe giggling fit. Realizing that I probably shouldn't be holding my son upside-down when I wasn't in the best physical condition, I returned him to his feet.

"How do you know?"

"I'm smart. I know everything. Roger, go grab the present, will you?"

I'd actually been joking, but Roger crutched his way over to the car and picked up the package. Nothing blew up and no knives shot out of the sides. We all got back in the car, and after a quick glance around to see if I could spot somebody walking away with wrapping paper and tape tucked under their arm, we drove home.

* * *

The kids had been sent to clean their rooms, which I figured would keep them busy for the next few dozen hours. Roger and I sat on the living room couch, while the present rested on the coffee table.

"So what do you think?" Roger asked. "It had to be either Dominick or Linda, right?"

I shrugged. "It's not tough to get a present on the hood of somebody's car. Everyone could have known we were going to be there today, so Carl or Farley could just as easily have been hanging around, too. And who's to say that The Apparition was the killer's only hired help? I don't think finding the present rules out anyone."

"Not even Rachel," said Roger. "She could have had Mr. Muscle put it there while we were distracted."

"Yes, but we're not going to discuss that." I leaned forward and tore off the bow. "Pretty big for a video tape."

"Plus it's too heavy for that to be the only thing in there."

"Are you sure you don't want to find a different continent to reside on while I open it?" I asked.

"Quit yapping and do it."

"I don't believe I've ever heard the word 'yapping' as part of your vocabulary before. Stress brings out odd things in people, I guess. I once knew this guy who got in a car accident and started to cluck like a—"

"Do it!"

I realized that I was babbling just to delay opening the package, so I apologized and ripped off the wrapping paper. This revealed a bare cardboard box. I used a knife I'd taken from the kitchen to slice through the tape on the lid, and raised the flaps.

Inside it was filled with confetti.

"Enough with the confetti," I muttered.

"Huh?"

"Sorry. There was confetti involved last night."

"And I missed it?"

I wasn't about to reach inside a potentially booby-trapped box and dig around for the tape, so I lifted it from the coffee table and poured the contents out onto the floor.

Confetti only accounted for about two inches on top. The next layer consisted of tacks.

"Good thing you didn't shove your face in there," Roger noted. "I had a really serious temptation to do that, and thank God I resisted."

"Har har." Next was a layer of those packing bubbles, which I can sit and pop for hours. I pulled that out and set it aside, revealing more confetti. There were probably more tacks under there, or something worse, so I dumped it out onto the floor with the rest.

"*Damn it!*" I shouted, as a quart-sized plastic sack of black ink tumbled out, landing on the tacks and splattering all over the carpet. The confetti blocked some of the ink, but not nearly enough.

I rushed into the bathroom and grabbed a stack of towels. Using the first towel as protection, I scooped up most of the tacks, then wadded up the towel and set it aside. I pushed the next towel tightly against the carpet, soaking up as much ink as possible, then repeated the procedure with the third and fourth towels. It wasn't wet anymore, but there was now a very large black splotch on our light gray carpet.

"I'm gonna kill him!" I said.

"Weren't those Helen's good towels?" Roger asked.

"She's gonna kill me!"

I picked up the towels and dumped them in the bathtub for the time being. I needed to focus on the problem at hand, not worry about the future agony to be inflicted upon me by my spouse. I returned to the living room, sat on the ruined carpet, and looked inside the box.

More confetti, but the corner of a videotape was sticking out. I took it out and saw a note taped to it, which I unfolded and read aloud:

"Dearest Andrew, I hope that your hands stop hurting, or that you didn't ruin anything expensive with the ink. I also hope that you enjoy this tape. I made it just for you. Watch carefully, because it will tell you who I am. Figure it out, and the game ends today. You get to be a hero. Have fun!"

"That sounds kind of promising," said Roger. "Maybe he's not such a bad psychopath after all."

I inserted the tape into the VCR and pressed "play," then sat next to Roger on the couch and turned on the television with the remote control.

We watched snow for about thirty seconds, and then a picture appeared. It looked like a setup for a puppet show, with a colorful wooden booth upon which was painted "The Gaggles and Boo-Boo Show!"

Cheery piano music began to play. The sound quality wasn't very good, as if it were coming from a tape player next to the microphone.

"Hey, kids!" said an excessively perky narrator. "Ghoulish Delights is pleased to present The Gaggles and Boo-Boo Show, starring your very best friends Gaggles and Boo-Boo!"

I couldn't recognize the voice for sure, but it kind of

sounded like The Apparition.

Two skulls popped into view from behind the stage. Each of them looked like a regular human skull, except that their teeth were filed into sharp fangs. One of them wore a cowboy hat.

"Hi, Gaggles!" The first skull's mouth began to move, and a comically high-pitched voice spoke for it.

"Hi, Boo-Boo!" said the second skull, the one with the hat. It sounded sort of like Grover from *Sesame Street*.

"How are you today, Gaggles?"

"I'm fine, Boo-Boo! What do you want to do today?"

"I don't know. What do *you* want to do today?"

This was really a sad excuse for theatre. Their mouths didn't even match the words, like some badly dubbed Japanese monster movie.

"I asked you first."

"I asked you second."

"Well, Boo-Boo, why don't we eat somebody?"

"That's a good idea, Gaggles! I love to eat people! Who shall we eat?"

"I know! Let's eat the woman tied to the bed in the next room! Won't that be fun?"

"That sure will! You're my very best friend, Gaggles."

"And you're my very best friend, Boo-Boo!"

"Shall we sing the Friendship Song?"

"Nah, fuck that. Let's just chow down on the bitch."

The camera panned over to the other side of the room, where a woman in shorts and a tank top was tied to the same bed as the man in the first video. I couldn't be positive, but I was pretty sure this was one of the women I'd seen at the end of that video. She had a blindfold over her eyes and a gag over her mouth, and struggled violently against the ropes.

Gaggles popped up in front of the camera. "Mmmmm. Looks tasty."

Boo-Boo joined him. "Very tasty."

"What should we eat first?"

"I'm in the mood for a drumstick."

The skulls dropped out of sight, and the camera moved in close to the woman's leg. It stayed there for almost a full minute, when suddenly Boo-Boo burst into view. I could see the hand controlling him—covered with a black glove like the hand in the first video. The skull's mouth opened wide, and then the sharpened fangs clamped down on the woman's thigh.

I turned down the volume several notches at the sound of her scream.

"Mmmmm...yum yum yum..." said Boo-Boo.

Roger turned his head away from the screen. I wanted to do the same, but the note said that the killer's identity would be revealed, and I couldn't afford to miss anything.

Gaggles soon joined his friend. Cold sweat poured down my sides, and my leg began shaking, but I kept watching, even as I felt a dizzy spell coming on.

It went on for over ten minutes, during which Roger took occasional looks at the screen and I kept my eyes firmly fixed on the picture. Every once in a while, one of the skulls would turn toward the camera and laugh. At one point, Gaggles disappeared from the scene and returned wearing a bib.

The woman died about two minutes before the end of it. There was no doubt whatsoever that she was dead. None.

Boo-Boo moved up to the camera, opening his bloody mouth wide. "That hit the spot! Nummy nummy!"

The cheerful piano music started up again. The perky narrator said "We hope you've enjoyed the adventures of Gaggles and Boo-Boo, best friends to the end! Good night, don't let the bed bugs bite, and don't forget to buy United States savings bonds! Bye-bye!"

The picture faded to black.

I staggered into the bathroom and threw up.

CHAPTER SIXTEEN

Roger and I each had a tall glass of ice water before we said anything. I guess this tape hadn't been much worse than the first, but seeing it on a large screen, in full color, with sound, made it much more disturbing.

"Was the other one like this?" asked Roger.

I nodded.

"And you actually watched a second one?"

"I didn't have much choice." I hit the fast forward button on the VCR remote to see if there was anything else on the tape. "But I sure didn't see the killer's name anywhere, did you?"

"Not unless he's named Gaggles or Boo-Boo."

"What about the voices? To me it sounded like The Apparition might have done all of them. What do you think?"

"I think you're probably right," said Roger. "Even if it wasn't him, it didn't sound like any of our other suspects, so that doesn't help."

"Well, there has to be a clue somewhere. We'll just have to keep watching the tape until we find it."

"So we're still not going to the police?"

"We can't. I have to believe that if the cops show up, he'll be able to kill the remaining prisoners before they can stop him. Or suppose the police are actually able to figure out who he is, and arrest him at the taping today...he might never tell where the prisoners are being kept. If he thinks he'll be dead soon and has nothing to lose, why would he? We just have to figure it out ourselves and trust that it'll really be over today."

"It could end with a slaughter," Roger pointed out.

I suddenly pressed the pause button. "Did you see that?"

"What?"

I rewound for a few seconds, catching a momentary glimpse of something on the television screen. I pressed play, and then watched until the message flashed on the screen, pausing the tape before it vanished again.

"Oooooh, this one's a toughie! Need an extra hint, Andrew? Go to 1214 Cruor Avenue. Alone, of course."

"Where's Cruor Avenue?" Roger asked.

"No idea." I pressed fast-forward again and watched the screen carefully in case more messages popped up.

"Are you going?"

"Not yet. Hopefully we won't need an extra hint if we can find out who he is from the rest of the tape."

We sat there for several minutes until the tape came to an end, with no other bonus hints that I noticed. I rewound the tape and we watched the section with Gaggles and Boo-Boo a second time. I paused it right before the first bite, not wanting to have to watch the torture again until I was sure the clue wasn't hidden in the introduction.

"What do you think?" Roger asked.

I sighed. "I'm not seeing anything that's pointing me in a specific direction. Maybe Gaggles and Boo-Boo are actual nicknames."

"What about the cowboy hat? That could mean something."

"It might," I agreed. "I wish there was some way we could safely get a copy of this to Rachel."

I suddenly had a paranoid mental image of somebody sitting outside in a van, listening to our conversation being transmitted from a bug that was hidden in the confetti. It was certainly possible. I hoped I hadn't doomed the rest of the prisoners.

We rewound the tape and watched a third time. I scooted up right against the screen, searching for hidden messages that might be in the background. Something about the way the skulls moved when they spoke seemed a little odd—odd beyond the way their mouths didn't match their words.

I pressed the mute button so their voices wouldn't be a distraction, and continued watching.

"Look at that," I said, tapping the screen on the skull with the cowboy hat. "Which one is this, Gaggles? Look how his mouth moves compared to Boo-Boo's."

Roger watched silently for a moment. "It definitely seems like two different people are working them."

"Right. Gaggles is a lot more haphazard. Boo-Boo almost looks like he's being controlled by a computer."

I thought about that. It was an interesting thing to notice, I guessed, but what was it supposed to mean?

Maybe two members of Ghoulish Delights were working together. Dominick and Linda, or Carl and Farley. Or, it could just be another helper like The Apparition. Either way, this observation did approximately squat in terms of revealing the killer's identity.

We rewound the tape yet again, but the fourth viewing provided no new insights. A fifth viewing had the same result.

So the clue we needed could very well be hidden after the skulls started their vicious work.

I really, truly, wholeheartedly did not want to watch that part of the video again, but I had to. Considering that real people had gone through the agonizing torture recorded on the tape, and to stop it from happening again all I had to do was sit in the comfort of my living room and watch it, I really had no excuse.

I watched the death of the woman in its entirety.

No clues presented themselves.

I looked over at the clock on the wall. Almost eight. Four hours until we needed to be at the taping.

"Okay, Roger," I said, "you're not going to like this, but I suggest you sit here and study the tape while I go to that Cruor place."

"All right, I'll see what I can do."

"And I assume you know to keep the doors locked and be alert for people stalking the house."

"You assumed correctly. But are you sure you really want to go there?"

I nodded. "I'll be okay. The killer has put me in some creepy situations since he dumped us in the ditch, but none of them were designed to put me in danger."

"So far. Be careful anyway."

"I will."

I went into Kyle's room and was pleased to discover that it was a full 2.5% cleaner than when he'd started. I did the usual hugs, kisses, descriptions of punishment should he not behave, and then proceeded into Theresa's room, which looked nearly 4% better. Maybe my parenting skills weren't so bad after all.

After telling Theresa that no, she couldn't come with me, I went outside, got in my car, and pulled a map of Chamber out of the glove compartment. I looked up Cruor Street on the sidebar index and saw that it was located in square B-7, which meant it was way on the other side of town. No big surprise.

* * *

Cruor Street was part of Richmond Heights. The "Rich" part of the name was appropriate, because this was the wealthiest section of town. I drove past house after house that made my place look like a rotting hovel until I reached 1214. It was a green two-story deal with a recently mowed lawn that had already been littered with toys. The roof was covered with three different antennas and a satellite dish. A car was parked in the driveway, but I couldn't tell what kind because it was hidden under one of those stupid car covers. It was probably a nice one, though.

I parked next to it, got out, and went up to the front porch and rang the doorbell.

"Hold on!" a voice called out. "I'll be there in a minute!"

It took about three minutes, but finally a well-tanned guy in his mid-forties opened the door. He wore denim shorts and a plain white t-shirt, had no remaining hair worth mentioning, and was in pretty good shape save for a small beer gut.

"May I help you?" he asked, smiling at me with perfect, unnaturally white teeth.

"This is going to be a bit unusual," I admitted, "but could I ask you a few questions?"

"No, I haven't been Saved," he said.

"Nothing like that."

"I don't need any magazine subscriptions, either."

"I'm not selling anything. Could I come inside?" I asked.

The man's smile faltered. "Is there some sort of problem?"

"You're not in any trouble or anything," I assured him. "I'm a private investigator, and I was hoping that maybe you might have some information for me."

Now the man looked downright uncomfortable. "I doubt I know anything. Are you sure this is the right house? Who are you looking for specifically?"

"Mr. Tandy." No great detective work there, I'd just checked the name on the mailbox.

"That's me, but I'm not sure what I can help you with."

"Have you heard of something called Ghoulish Delights?"

The man shook his head. "No. Never." He was so obviously lying that it was almost comical.

"Are you sure? Because it's my understanding that some very high-level people are looking for a Mr. Tandy in conjunction with Ghoulish Delights."

His tan seemed to pour right off of his face as he whitened. "Maybe you should come inside."

"Thank you."

We stepped into the living room, which was filled with furniture that consisted of either wildly expensive antiques or old junk—I couldn't tell which. He pulled the door shut behind me and gestured to the couch. "Please, have a seat. My wife and kids should be back any minute, so I'd appreciate it if you could make this quick," he said. "Can I get you something to drink?"

I wasn't in the mood to chug down an arsenic-laced lemonade or a root beer filled with razor blades, so I politely declined and sat down. I sank so far down into the cushion that for a second I almost thought it was some sort of death trap.

Mr. Tandy sat down on the fading recliner. "Now, what did you say you were wanting to know about?"

"Ghoulish Delights."

"And what is Ghoulish Delights supposed to be?"

"You know darn well what it is," I said, giving him my own version of The Gaze.

"I'm sorry, I don't."

"Does the name Michael Ashcraft mean anything to you?"

"No."

"What about Jennifer Ashcraft?"

"No."

"Okay, then how about Victor Grunge? He's a six-foot-eight, three-hundred-fifty pound horndog currently sitting in the Chamber Jail waiting for a new cellmate to replace the one he broke last night."

"You're not intimidating me," said Mr. Tandy, wiping about a quart of sweat off his forehead.

"*Boo!*"

Mr. Tandy jumped a good two inches off his seat.

"I think I am," I said.

"I swear, I don't know anything about any Ghoulish Delights. I don't know where you're getting your information, but it's wrong. I'm afraid I'm going to have to ask you to leave."

"I believe I'll stay."

"Okay." Mr. Tandy stared at the floor for a moment, and then began to check his fingernails for dirt.

I figured there were two ways that this guy could be involved. He was either working for the killer, or he was a Ghoulish Delights customer. And he seemed far too jittery to be a worthwhile employee, so I suspected it was the latter.

"Let me lay it all on the line," I said, leaning forward and looking him right in the eye. "I know that you have been purchasing a series of tapes depicting extended torture and vicious murders that are, how should I put it, not simulated. Am I correct?"

"No! I don't know what you're talking about."

"Oh, really? Mind if I take a look around?"

"Do you have a search warrant?"

"I can get one."

"You can not. You said you were a private investigator, not a cop."

"I say lots of things to lots of people," I told him, mentally giving myself a solid kick in the butt for the search warrant gaffe. "And what I'm saying to you now is, you'd better tell me everything you know or you'll find yourself locked away from your wife and children for a long, long time."

"But I didn't do anything!"

"Then how about telling me what exactly it is you *didn't* do?"

"Nothing! I mean, everything! I mean...you know what I

mean! I didn't do anything!"

"Do you want to hear what happened to Victor's last cellmate?"

"No!"

"It was mop city afterward, let me tell you."

Mr. Tandy stood up. "I said I don't know anything, and I'd like you to leave my house right now."

"Fine," I said. "I hope you've got your passport ready, because you'll be wanting to flee the country before the day is over. You're busted, Mr. Tandy, so I'd advise you to make it easy for yourself. Tell me what you know."

He sat back down and buried his face in his hands. "I don't know anything. I swear."

"You don't swear very convincingly."

He remained motionless for a moment, then removed his hands and looked up at me with wet eyes. "I didn't buy a series of tapes. Only one. That's all."

"And who did you buy it from?"

"Michael Ashcraft. I swear to you, I didn't hurt anyone! They did everything! All I did was fill out a form." Mr. Tandy's voice cracked. "That's all I did. I only watched. I didn't touch anyone."

"What was on the form?"

"You know, hair color, age, race, build..."

"Yours?"

Mr. Tandy stifled a sob. "No, for the victim I wanted."

Oh dear Lord, I thought. Snuff films made to order.

It was all I could do to keep from walking over and punching the sick bastard in the face. But I remained calm, even as Mr. Tandy broke down completely.

"I swear, I didn't hurt her! They said I could help out, participate if I wanted, or maybe watch the whole thing live and keep the tape as a souvenir, but I didn't! I wasn't there! All I did was watch the tape! I didn't tell them who to kidnap!"

"And how much did you pay for the privilege of watching somebody die?" I asked.

"One hundred thousand dollars," Mr. Tandy replied in a quiet, almost inaudible voice.

"Well, I'm glad you're doing so well for yourself," I said. "That's a pretty big chunk of money for a tape, when you can rent *Faces of Death* for a couple of bucks at 7th Street Video.

I guess even though you didn't kill her yourself, it gave you a nice little tingle knowing that she was dying because of you." I looked him over carefully, pretending to study him to figure out what his tastes might be. "Let me guess...you picked a redhead, maybe eighteen years old, athletic build, right?"

"No. She was forty. Brown hair. Heavyset."

"Well, to each his own." I cracked my knuckles. "Listen, what I should do is beat the shit out of you then haul you straight to the police station. But I'm not going to. In fact, things may work out all right for you, if you're willing to play along."

Of course, once the prisoners were safe I was going to make sure this guy was put away for a long time. But he'd find that out later.

"What do I have to do?"

"First off, you know the hundred grand you paid for that video? You're going to pay me twice that to keep quiet." If he thought I was nothing more than a blackmailer, he wouldn't question why I was letting him go.

Mr. Tandy nodded. "I don't have the money now. You don't know how hard it was to get it the first time without my wife knowing."

"You have exactly one week to get it. Remember, I know where you live. Now, I have some questions that I want answered."

Suddenly Mr. Tandy's eyes widened. "My wife's just pulled up! You've got to leave!"

"I'm not going anywhere," I said. "Tell her I'm an old friend, then we'll find someplace to talk in private."

Mr. Tandy lifted the bottom of his shirt and used it to wipe his eyes. The door opened and a woman entered, with three grade-school kids behind her, the youngest holding a box of doughnuts. I almost had to laugh when I saw her.

About forty. Brown hair. Heavyset.

"Oh, hello," she said to me. Her pleasant expression switched to one of concern as she noticed Mr. Tandy's distraught condition. "Ben, is something wrong?"

Mr. Tandy shook his head unconvincingly.

"I apologize for disturbing you," I told her. "I'm just here to speak with your husband about a financial matter. Nothing for you to worry about."

"I handle most of the finances," Mrs. Tandy said. "Should I be speaking with you as well?"

"No, I think we've got most of it covered. Really, it's nothing to concern yourself over."

Mr. Tandy stood up. "I'll be back in a second. I need to use the bathroom."

"Kids, go play outside," said Mrs. Tandy, ushering them out into the front yard. "Ben, are you sure you're okay?"

"I'm fine. Yes."

He walked into the hallway, moving like one of the living dead. I wanted to keep him in sight, but what was I going to do, tell him he couldn't take a leak? I heard the bathroom door close and turned to face Mrs. Tandy.

"What's going on?" she asked.

"It's a personal matter."

"I'm his wife. We don't have secrets."

Oh, was she in for a bit of a shock.

"I'm sorry, but this is between Ben and I. Whatever he wants to tell you, he can."

"I expect him to tell me everything. I hope you understand that it's very upsetting to come home and find a total stranger in my house and my husband looking like he's ready to kill himself."

Forget letting the man urinate in peace. I rushed down the hallway and pounded on the only closed door.

"Mr. Tandy, open up!"

"Go away!"

"I mean it. Open the door. We need to finish talking."

Mrs. Tandy walked into the hallway after me, wringing her hands in what seemed more like agitation than nervousness. "What the hell is going on?"

I tested the doorknob. Unlocked. I threw open the door, figuring that it was well worth the risk of embarrassment if he happened to be merely sitting on the toilet.

He wasn't.

He was standing at the sink, a razor in his hand.

CHAPTER SEVENTEEN

He'd taken a regular plastic shaver and broken the top to get at the blade, which he held pinched between his thumb and index finger.

"Stay away!" he said.

I rushed him, and he flung the razor at me. It bounced harmlessly off my chest as I grabbed him and easily pinned his arms behind his back. Mrs. Tandy screamed.

"Be quiet!" I shouted at her. "Don't make a sound! Now listen to me, I need your full cooperation, both of you! I'm only here to ask questions, nothing else! I just need you to—"

Mrs. Tandy vanished from sight, and I heard her footsteps running down the hall, probably toward the nearest phone. I shoved Mr. Tandy out of the way. His leg struck the bathtub and he fell to the floor. The razor was still on the floor, within his reach, so I gave it a good kick then followed his wife to stop her before she called the police.

I hurried down the hall, through the living room, and into the kitchen, where Mrs. Tandy stood next to a phone mounted on the wall. She held the handset in one hand and was punching buttons with the other.

I grabbed the phone from her and gave the cord a good yank, popping it out of the jack. "Do you want your husband to die?" I demanded. "Do you?"

She shook her head, tears spilling down her face. "No!"

"Then sit down and stay calm! If you don't do as I say you might as well slice his wrists yourself!"

I couldn't believe I'd said something like that, but this was no time for compassion. I sprinted back into the bathroom, ready for the sight of Mr. Tandy lying on the tile in a pool of blood, his wrists slashed wide open.

But he hadn't gone for the razor. He was sitting against the bathtub, his eyes vacant. "Why can't you leave me alone?" he asked.

"I'm sorry if I'm inconveniencing you," I said. "I know what a pain it is when somebody shows up uninvited and exposes you for the twisted deviant that you are."

"You just don't understand."

"No, I don't, and thank God for that. But here's your chance to redeem yourself. I need names. Besides Michael Ashcraft, who is involved in making the tapes?"

Mr. Tandy shrugged.

"Look, man, if you don't want your face plastered all over the front page of tomorrow's newspaper, you'll answer my questions. Now who's involved?"

"It was his wife," Mr. Tandy said. "And some other guy."

"What other guy?"

"He never told me his name."

"What did he look like?"

"Sort of creepy. Old guy. Big white beard."

Great. The Apparition. No help at all.

"Who else?"

"Nobody else."

"You're lying. There's somebody else working for Ghoulish Delights that you haven't told me about."

Mr. Tandy's voice abruptly switched from a pained whisper to a shout. "What do you think, they took me around and introduced me to everyone? *I don't know who you're talking about!* All I did was order the tape. That's all."

"Where'd they get the girl?"

He lowered his voice again. "I don't know! All they said was that they take people who won't be missed. Maybe she was homeless. I didn't ask. Why are you asking me all this stuff instead of bugging Michael Ashcraft? He's the one you should be talking to! I didn't do anything!"

I noticed Mrs. Tandy standing in the hallway, staring at

us as her hands shook. I shut the bathroom door in her face.

"I don't care what you did or didn't do," I told Mr. Tandy. "You're the one I'm talking to."

"But I don't *know* anything!"

"How did you find out about Ghoulish Delights?"

"The Internet. A chat room."

"Must've been some chat," I said with a dry chuckle.

"Hey, you don't know anything about me! You have no right to stand here acting all haughty and arrogant!"

"I'm going to make two points. One, 'haughty' and 'arrogant' mean the same thing. Two, because of you an innocent woman was tortured to death. I don't need to know anything about you to figure out that there's something seriously wrong with you."

Mr. Tandy buried his face in his hands and began sobbing. His shoulders shook, his head bobbed, and after a couple of minutes of trying to calm him down I had to accept that I wasn't going to get anything out of him.

I opened the bathroom door. Mrs. Tandy stood there, her face pale and tight. "Please, tell me what's going on."

I ignored her and walked toward the front door. I knew the secret behind Ghoulish Delights now, but I couldn't see how this was supposed to help me find the hidden clues in the video.

As I stepped outside, I saw an envelope taped to the passenger door of my car. Forget searching for leads and interviewing suspects...I needed to just stay in my damn car all day!

I hurried over to the car, glanced around to catch a glimpse of the delivery person I knew would be nowhere in sight, then ripped open the envelope. It felt like it contained several pieces of paper. I have to admit, I was feeling pretty darn uncomfortable hanging around here, and I really didn't know what Mr. Tandy might be capable of, so I got in my car and sped off.

I drove out of the neighborhood and pulled into the parking lot of a small library, then carefully opened the envelope and removed its contents.

Five pieces of notebook paper.

One Trojan-brand condom. Ribbed.

I didn't even want to know what the condom was for yet, so I looked over the first piece of paper. In crayon, in a child's scrawl, was the following letter:

"Dear Gramma, I miss you. Arizona is fun. Mom sed that

I could have all the soda I want during the trip. I love you. XOXOXO. Love, Amy."

The next letter was similar:

"Dear Gramma, I miss you. Its hot hear but I still lik it. We will be back soon. I love you. XOXOXO. Love, Amy."

There were three more letters, all to Gramma from Amy, all to basically the same effect.

Five letters and a condom. And somehow this was supposed to tie in with the tape.

I held open the envelope and looked inside to make sure I hadn't missed anything. And I had. A message written on the inside of the envelope read: "One after the creation of the other."

Huh?

I tore open the foil wrapper to make sure there was nothing else of importance hidden inside the condom. As I removed the condom and examined it, a woman walking past the car with an armload of books noticed me and picked up her pace. Looked like a normal condom. The kind I no longer had to wear ever since the birth of Kyle, when Helen decided that our child quota had been met and it was time for me to get a...but that's bringing up a horrible memory I don't want to discuss.

I unrolled the condom completely just in case the killer had written some sort of message on it, but no, it still looked like your standard-issue prophylactic. Wow, these things were huge when you unrolled them all the way.

Satisfied that this condom was in fact a regular condom, I rolled it back up as well as I could and stuffed it back into the wrapper. I returned all of the parts of the clue to the envelope, and began to drive home.

One after the creation of the other.

Wasn't the whole purpose of a condom to *prevent* creation? So "creation" had to refer to the letters.

A condom after the creation of the letters.

Was Arizona the important part? Or maybe it was the misspelled words, such as "sed" and "lik."

One after the creation of the other.

I was completely baffled.

Then my heart rate doubled as I saw the red and blue lights flashing in my rear-view mirror.

CHAPTER EIGHTEEN

Oh, this was bad. This was really bad.

I glanced around quickly and saw that there were no other cars near me. The flashing lights on that police car were meant for me, and me only.

What was I supposed to do? If the killer or one of his flunkies was watching and saw me talking to a cop, that might blow the whole deal. Even if they were listening in somehow and I didn't say anything suspicious, they'd probably assume I'd relayed a message some other way.

I briefly considered flooring the gas pedal and testing my car chase skills, but quickly decided that would be a bad idea. If I got caught, I'd be taken in to the station, and then the prisoners would be doomed for certain. Besides, the officer had probably already noted my license plate number.

Wonderful. Just wonderful.

I pulled over to the side of the road and killed the engine. I looked up in the rear-view mirror and ran a hand through my hair. God, I looked terrible. The combination of big-time stress and lack of sleep gave me the appearance of an intoxicated zombie. Bloodshot eyes, bruises, rumpled clothes...I looked like somebody that any local cop would want to throw out of his town.

I rolled down my window as the officer approached. Naturally, he was tall, had a muscular build, and facial features that looked carved out of stone. Naturally, he had an expression that said "I've had a lousy day and I'm in the mood to stomp somebody."

Naturally, I patted my jeans and realized that with all the distractions this morning, I'd forgotten to bring my wallet.

The officer stopped at the door and leaned down toward the window. He had to lean a long way. "May I see your license, registration, and proof of insurance, please?"

"Yes, sir," I said, opening the glove compartment. I thought about how interesting it would be if another hand dropped out, but there was only the usual assortment of receipts, useless papers, and various junk so jam-packed in there that it took a full two minutes to locate my registration and the auto insurance card. I handed it over. "I'm sorry, but I left in a hurry and forgot my wallet at home."

"Did you, now?"

"Yes. I can tell you right where it is on the kitchen counter, if that helps." I tried to smile.

"That won't be necessary." The officer looked me over carefully. "Do you know why I pulled you over?"

"No, sir."

"When you made that left turn after leaving the library, you failed to signal. That's very dangerous to other drivers, who cannot be expected to anticipate your moves."

"Oh, that's right. I'm sorry. I'm just tired, I guess."

"Perhaps if you're that tired you shouldn't be driving at all. Some rest would probably do you good."

I nodded. "I was on my way home."

"I see. Returning some overdue library books, were you?"

"Yes."

"I see. Please wait here in your car."

The officer walked back to the squad car and got inside, presumably to check on my registration and insurance information. I wiped my sweaty hands off on my jeans and tried to breathe calmly. If I played it cool, everything might work out fine. The killer might not even be watching.

I nervously drummed my fingers on the steering wheel.

A few minutes later, the officer returned. "Are you Mr. Andrew Mayhem?"

"Yes, sir."

"And this is your car?"

"Yes, sir."

"Do you have any sort of picture I.D. on you?"

"No, I don't."

"Mind telling me how you got those bruises?"

The bruises? Well, you see, after digging up this guy who turned out to not really be dead, some psychopath hit me in the head with a chain and then tied me to a chair and punched me a couple of times. Yes, I know, it seemed a bit odd to me at the time, too.

"Two-by-four," I said. "My friend was carrying one on his shoulder when he spun around to look at something. Bashed me in the face."

"You should tell your friend to be more careful."

"Oh, I did, believe me."

"That's the whole problem. I *don't* believe you."

"Sir, I realize how bad I look," I said. "It's been a really rough couple of days. And I'm sorry I don't have my driver's license with me—things have just been so hectic that I forgot it. I don't know what I need to do to convince you that I am Andrew Mayhem and this is my car, but tell me what it is and I'll do it."

"Are you attempting to bribe me?"

"What? No! I don't even have my wallet!"

"I'm afraid I'll have to ask you to come with me to the station until somebody can verify your identity."

"That's not necessary, I'll—"

"Don't you tell me what is and what isn't necessary. I'm not completely convinced that this *is* your automobile, sir."

"When you checked my registration, was it reported stolen?"

"That's none of your business. Please step out of the car."

"I can't do that."

"Step out of the car immediately or you will be placed under arrest."

"Look, it's crucial that you listen to me. You can't take me in! Five...no, four people will die if you do!"

At this, the officer drew his revolver from its holster. "Place your hands on the steering wheel where I can see them."

I did so. "*I'm* not going to kill them, there's somebody else! I don't know who it is, but if you take me in he'll do it!"

The officer opened the door. "Step out of the vehicle," he

said, pointing the gun at me. *"Right now."*

"Please, you have to—."

"NOW!"

I unfastened my seat belt and got out of the car.

"Put your hands flat on the vehicle and keep your legs apart."

I did as I was told. The officer frisked me, and then snapped a pair of handcuffs on me. He grabbed me by the shirt collar and began to lead me toward the squad car.

"Wait!" I protested. "There's an envelope on the car seat! I need it!"

"It will still be there when you pick up the car from impound. You have the right to remain silent. Anything you say can and will be used against you in a court of law."

"You have to listen to me!"

"Quiet! You have the right to an attorney. If you cannot afford an attorney..."

* * *

I quickly figured out that the officer wasn't interested in anything I had to say, so I kept my mouth shut during the drive to the police station.

Well, I'd screwed things up pretty thoroughly. If the prisoners weren't dead already, they soon would be. And I didn't even want to think about how much trouble I was personally in.

If this all blew over, I was getting myself a real job. Nine to five. I'd even wear a tie. I might wear a wacky one with cartoon characters once in a while, but damn it, I'd wear a tie.

I went through the booking procedure, got a couple of photos taken (at least with a mug shot I knew I wouldn't have my usual will-you-hurry-up-and-take-the-damn-picture-already smile), and was fingerprinted.

"Listen to me," I told the officer who was doing my fingerprints. He was a younger guy, barely looked old enough to be a college student. "I absolutely have to talk to somebody right away. I don't care who...any cop you've got is fine. But I cannot stress enough how vital it is that I explain what's going on. Some people will be killed. Maybe they already have been. Do you understand?"

"I'll see what I can do," he said, leading me over to a very tidy desk upon which rested a telephone. "You get one phone call, but make it quick."

I dialed my home number. "Hello?" said Kyle.

"Kyle, this is Daddy. Could you put Roger on the phone?"

"He's not here."

"What do you mean, he's not there?"

"He's in the bathroom."

"Knock on the door and tell him it's important, okay?"

"'Kay."

There was a loud *thump* in my ear and I flinched.

"Daddy?"

"Yes, Kyle?"

"The phone fell. I'll go get Roger."

A moment later Roger got on the line. "Andrew, what's up?"

"I've been arrested."

"Are you serious? You're kidding, right?"

"No. I'm at the police station."

"Aw, shit!"

"I need you to come down here and prove that I'm really Andrew Mayhem. Grab my wallet off the counter. Helen's keys are hanging up in the kitchen, you can take her car."

"All right. Did you find out anything when you went to that place?"

"I found what I was supposed to, but I don't have any idea what it means yet. Before you come to the station, I need you to drive to the Southview branch of the library. My car is parked a couple blocks away...I don't remember the street, but it's a left turn after you pull out of the parking lot. I've got a spare car key hanging on the hook next to the refrigerator, so you can use that to get inside and grab the envelope that's on the seat. You have to hurry because they'll be sending a tow truck to take it away."

"No problem. Anything else?"

"Yeah, bring the tape. But don't show yourself outside with it. Have Theresa carry her bookbag, and put it in there."

"The other tape's still at my place. Should I get it?"

"No. They might be watching your house."

"Okay. We'll be there as soon as possible."

"Thanks, buddy."

I hung up. When I turned around, the young officer was standing there with a pair of black cops. They were both about forty, heavyset, bald, had thick mustaches, and were identical twins.

"These are Sergeants Frenkle and Frenkle. They'll hear what you have to say."

* * *

I'd never been in a real interrogation room before, and this one looked just like those I'd seen in the movies. A long table, uncomfortable chairs, bright white lights, everything.

I told them the truth, the whole truth, and nothing but the truth. Except that I left out the people's names.

Now, I could have waited for Roger to show up with my I.D., convinced them that I was merely some tired driver who forgot to signal, and then left. But if the killer knew I'd been arrested, he'd naturally assume that I'd spilled my guts, whether I really did or not. So if I was going to be penalized anyway, I decided I might as well talk to them. It's not like I'd been able to figure things out all by myself. Might as well let them have a shot.

I also considered leaving out the graverobbing, but quite honestly I was too mentally exhausted to come up with a good cover story as to how I'd become involved. And I didn't want them to catch me in any inconsistencies. Better to tell the whole truth and worry about the consequences later.

"That's quite a story," said Sergeant Tony Frenkle, who was distinguishable from his brother Bruce only by a small mole above his left eyebrow.

"If it's an excuse to get out of a traffic ticket, it's the best one I've ever heard," said Bruce.

"Do you believe me?" I asked.

Tony shrugged. "Not really. But you say your friend is on his way with the tape, so we'll have a look at it together and see if that changes things."

I checked my watch. Twenty minutes since I'd called Roger. He'd be here any second, as long as Theresa and Kyle weren't giving him any problems.

"Please, you have to promise me that you're not going to do any investigating," I said. "He'll kill them."

"Your story isn't leaving this room for the time being,"

Tony assured me. "I am, to get some coffee, but your story stays here."

"Thank you."

Bruce asked me some to clarify some parts of the story while we waited for Tony to return. When he did, it was with three cups of the worst coffee I'd ever tasted. The stuff made my tongue want to leap out of my mouth and never return.

"While we're waiting, why don't you tell us your story again, to make sure we've got everything straight?" suggested Bruce. What he meant was, tell us the story again so we can try to catch you in a lie.

So I told them the story again.

After about ten minutes, I was starting to get a bit nervous. What was taking Roger so long?

After thirty minutes, I was more than nervous. I was frantic.

After an hour, I was terrified.

CHAPTER
NINETEEN

After another fifteen minutes, there was a knock on the door. Bruce answered it and stepped outside to speak with somebody. Less than a minute later he returned.

"Your friend, his name is Roger Tanglen, right?"

"Yes! Is he here? Does he have my kids?"

"Maybe you should come with me."

"Why? What happened?"

"Just come with me."

I followed Bruce and another cop out into the front area of the police station. Tony walked close behind us. I made every effort to think positive thoughts, even though a voice in my head kept shrieking that my children were dead.

As we walked through the front door I saw about five cops crowded around something in the parking lot, partially blocking it from my view. We hurried over to the crowd as the policeman who'd spoken to Bruce shouted for them to clear a path. The cops stepped aside to let us through, revealing what they were gathered around.

Roger.

He was standing against a large plank of wood, about the size of a door. In fact, it probably *was* a door. Bands fastened his legs at the ankles, and another band wrapped around his neck.

His eyes were wide and frightened. Duct tape over his

mouth looked like it was wrapped all the way around his head. Above his head, neon orange letters proclaimed that this was "The Dismemberment Game!" Smaller letters in black magic marker said "Starring Roger Tanglen and Andrew Mayhem." A note taped to Roger's chest read "Pigs, stay away! This is Andrew's game."

Fixed to the door were six machete blades, the flat edge of each blade on the wood. The bottom of each blade was attached to a mechanism that was clearly designed to swing it. A blade on each side of his head was positioned to lop off his arms at the shoulder, while blades on each side of his waist were positioned to lop off his legs. A blade next to his right shoulder was set to decapitate him. The sixth blade was at the very bottom of the door, resting on the pavement perpendicular to the door. Between Roger's legs there was an enormous slab of raw meat, probably a cow flank.

"Oh dear Lord..." whispered Tony.

"All right, everyone back!" shouted Bruce, waving his arms. "Clear some space! We need anything solid we could use to block those knives!"

I walked up to the door. "Can anyone get a chainsaw or something to cut him free?"

The officer closest to the door shook his head. "Look at the back."

I did so. From behind, I could see that the door was propped up by two pieces of wood at the bottom. The entire back of the door was a maze of what must have been thousands of multi-colored wires. Connected to the door by several other wires was a laptop computer, which the cop who'd taken my fingerprints currently had balanced on his palm.

"We don't know which one of those wires will spring the machete blades," said the fingerprint cop. "If we cut the wrong one, it could go off." He extended the laptop toward me. "Take this. It's for you."

I took the laptop from him and looked at the low-resolution, black-and-white display. "GET ANDREW MAYHEM, THEN PRESS ANY KEY. YOU HAVE 43 SECONDS REMAINING." The countdown continued.

"Don't press it yet," said the fingerprint cop. "We need as much time as possible to figure out a way to get him out of this."

The wires were long enough that I could walk around to the front of the door while still holding the laptop. I looked up at Roger and asked "He's got Kyle and Theresa, hasn't he?"

Roger gave me a small nod, and then closed his eyes.

Only sixteen seconds remained on the display. I couldn't panic. I couldn't lose it. I had to stay calm, focus, and make everything all right.

When only three seconds remained, I pressed the space bar. A new message appeared: "ENTER YOUR MOTHER'S MAIDEN NAME."

With my free hand I typed in KENDALL and hit return.

"BAD BOY, ANDREW. I SAID NO COPS. I'D PLANNED TO SAVE THIS GAME FOR A LITTLE LATER, BUT YOU'VE FORCED ME TO RUSH THINGS. TOO BAD FOR YOU. AND ROGER."

The screen went blank, then a new message appeared. "YOU MUST ANSWER FIVE QUESTIONS CORRECTLY. EACH TIME YOU MISS, ROGER LOSES AN APPENDAGE."

"My God, who *is* this guy?" asked Tony, looking at the screen.

"I don't know."

The number 10 appeared at the bottom of the screen, and went down by one with each passing second. "PRACTICE QUESTION. WHO WAS THE TWELFTH PRESIDENT OF THE UNITED STATES?"

"Who was our twelfth president?" I shouted. The cops began discussing it amongst themselves, and one counted on his fingers while reciting names.

"Hurry! I only have three seconds!"

"Tyler!" said the guy counting on his fingers. "No, no, Taylor! Zachary Taylor!"

I typed in T-A-Y...

"TIME'S UP."

The bottom machete blade swung upward like an enormous mousetrap going off. It split through the meat and smashed into the wood with a loud *thunk*! The top of the blade came less than an inch from splitting Roger's jeans and the sensitive parts beneath them. Then it swung back and returned to its original position.

There was a gasp of shock from the crowd of police officers. Roger's eyes were closed so tightly that his head looked ready to burst.

"QUESTION ONE. RIGHT ARM. WHICH SKULL WEARS THE COWBOY HAT?"

Which one? Gaggles or Boo-Boo? I couldn't remember!

No, it had been Gaggles, right?

Five seconds remained. No time to replay the video in my mind. I typed GAGGLES and hit enter.

"CORRECT. RIGHT ARM SPARED."

I let myself breathe a sigh of relief.

"QUESTION TWO. LEFT ARM. WHICH SKULL BIT FIRST?"

I definitely knew this one. Boo-Boo.

I typed in BOO-BOO. Enter.

"CORRECT. LEFT ARM SPARED."

If they were all questions from the video, I could handle this. I'd certainly been paying attention when I watched it.

"QUESTION THREE. RIGHT LEG. WERE THERE MORE OR FEWER THAN FIFTY BITES THAT KILLED THE WOMAN ON THE BED?"

I didn't know! Possibly more than fifty, but I hadn't counted.

I typed in MORE. Hesitated for a couple of seconds. Then hit return.

"CORRECT. FIFTY-EIGHT, TO BE EXACT. RIGHT LEG SPARED."

If that question ever popped up on *Jeopardy* I'd be set.

"QUESTION FOUR. LEFT LEG. IN MULTIPLES OF FIVE MINUTES, HOW LONG DOES IT TAKE TO CLEAN UP AFTER THE AVERAGE GHOULISH DELIGHTS MURDER-ON-TAPE?"

How the hell was I supposed to know that?

"Give that here!" said Tony to someone behind me. As he walked up to the door, I saw that he held a metal pipe, about two feet long. Bruce stepped forward and each of them took an end. "Left leg, correct?" he asked me.

"Correct!" Three seconds remained on the timer.

I typed 60 and at the last second hit enter.

"WRONG. THE CORRECT ANSWER IS 45. LEFT LEG SEVERED."

The blade positioned by his left leg swung with incredible force, striking the metal pipe with a loud *clang*. Bruce and Tony both let out a grunt as the pipe was wrenched out of their grasp. It slammed against Roger's leg with a sound that had to be bone breaking. Roger let out a muffled cry of pain.

The blade swung back to its original position.

Roger was badly hurt, but at least he still had his leg.

"FINAL QUESTION. NECK."

"The next one's going for his neck!" I shouted. Bruce and Tony quickly positioned the pipe so that it would block the blade, and two other cops joined to help them hold it.

"WHO AM I?"

If I knew that, I wouldn't have been in this situation to begin with! Carl, Farley, Dominick, Linda...maybe even Rachel...who could it be? I had a one in five chance of guessing correctly.

One in four, if I discounted Rachel.

Even if the pipe stopped the blade from cutting him, if I got this wrong my best friend was going to end up with a broken neck.

Five seconds.

I typed in CARL.

Three seconds.

I placed my finger over the enter key.

Two seconds.

No! The odds were too much against me!

Better to try something where I didn't *know* the odds.

I spun around and flung the laptop into the air as hard as I could. The wires connecting it to the door snapped.

The bottom blade snapped up, slamming into the wood between Roger's legs again.

A split-second later, the blade to the right of Roger's waist sprung. The cops spun the pipe downward, and the bottom of it passed in front of Roger's right leg an instant before the blade hit. Though there were four cops holding it, the pipe was still wrenched away from them, and crunched against Roger's leg in the same area as before, but at a new angle. Roger shrieked beneath the tape.

The blade to the left of Roger's waist sprung, slamming against the opposite blade.

The blade on the right side of Roger's head, the one intended to chop off his right arm, sprung, coming down upon the upper end of the pipe and crushing it into his shoulder. It was immediately followed by the blade on the left side of his head, which struck the right blade and elicited another shriek from Roger.

The blade aimed at Roger's neck sprung. It connected with the other two blades, giving the pipe against his shoulder a third slam.

And that was it.

Roger remained fastened to the door, probably with a shattered leg and shoulder. But he still had his head. He'd live.

"We need some saws and a metal cutter!" shouted Bruce, but somebody had already retrieved the metal-cutting shears. While the cop with the shears went to work on the band around Roger's right leg, Tony pulled out a pocketknife and began to cut through the duct tape.

He ripped the tape away from Roger's mouth, and Roger spoke in a weak voice. "Under my shirt...an envelope..."

I lifted his shirt to reveal an envelope folded into quarters and taped to his chest. I pulled it off, tore it open, and read the letter inside.

"So, how does your friend look without his head? Sorry that there was no correct answer to the last question, but I couldn't give anything away in case you made a lucky guess. You're probably wondering what happened to your kids. Are they still alive? Did I chop their heads off, too? Nope, not yet. I'll save that for later, unless you cooperate. We'll consider your involvement with the cops an unfortunate little detour that cost your friend his life. If you ever want your kids back, you'll proceed exactly as planned. Go home and relax, then come to the taping. Join the fun. Try to solve the mystery. Otherwise I'll get to add a new age bracket to the list of *Ghoulish Delights* stars. So you make sure those pigs stay out of it. I have insiders on the force, so don't try anything remotely sneaky. If I get the slightest bit suspicious, your son and daughter will be screaming in pain for days, and they'll be dead for months before you find them. Got it? Good."

I touched my hand to my cheek. I hadn't even realized I was crying.

"I'm so sorry, Andrew..." said Roger. They were having trouble getting the metal band off his arm, and it didn't look like he'd be free anytime soon. "I didn't see it coming."

"Do you know who it was?"

"No. I was knocked out with something, and when I came to I was in the back of a van. I couldn't see who was doing it...I was just dumped off here."

"Was it more than one person?"

"I don't think so. They used a cart or something, so one person could have done it alone."

I turned toward the crowd of police officers. "I have to go home," I said. "I have to find the person who did this on my own. He has my kids and he has four other prisoners. If he thinks there's any police involvement, any at all, he'll kill them. He doesn't want anyone else playing his game."

"That's crazy," said Bruce. "You've got it narrowed down to five suspects. We'll just round 'em up and bring 'em in!"

"No! If he sees any cops, my kids are dead! He'll kill them before you finish knocking!"

"We at least can have people keep an eye on you," said Tony. "Plainclothes cops. They'll blend in. He'll never know they're there."

I shook my head. "Please, you've got to stay completely out of this. All of you." I pointed to The Dismemberment Game. "Look at what kind of stuff this guy sets up! I mean, do you honestly believe he'll hesitate to kill my children? I don't know what his resources are, I don't know who he has working for him, I don't know anything except that if there is *any* police involvement in this matter, there's a really good chance that I'll never see my kids alive again. Please, let me do what I have to do."

A middle-aged man in gray pants and a rumpled dress shirt stepped forward. "My name is James Geldern, Chamber County Chief of Police. We'll get your friend out of there. Go get your kids."

"I mean it, you can't have me followed," I insisted.

"We won't have you followed. The mind that created a contraption like this is not the kind of mind I want to make angry. Now get the hell off police property before something like this happens again."

"Thank you." I looked at Roger. "You'll be okay, don't worry."

"I'm sorry, Andrew...I tried to do something but I..."

"Forget about it. It wasn't your fault."

I walked away from the police parking lot and onto the sidewalk. Theresa and Kyle would be okay. Everything would turn out okay. It had to.

In my mind I heard the delighted cackle of a wicked witch. *"Would you like to see my little puppet show, dearies? Fifty-eight bites between the two of you! Don't forget, my puppets love it when you screeeeeeeaaaaaaaaam."*

CHAPTER TWENTY

Two blocks from the police station I reached a pay phone. It had to be safe to call a cab...the killer couldn't expect me to spend a couple of hours walking home. After being told the cab would be there in about ten minutes, I leaned against the brick wall of a hardware store and waited.

Sharpened skull fangs, digging into Kyle's leg...

No! That wasn't going to happen!

I had to put my kids out of my mind and focus on the problem. Focus on the riddle.

One after the creation of the other.

Letters to grandma and a condom.

What did a letter create? Happiness. Knowledge. Waste paper. What else? A letter *was* a creation, not something that created.

What could possibly be the creation of a condom, besides something icky to throw away after it was used? A sense of security? A sense of protection?

How could any of this relate to the video?

I kicked the wall in frustration.

Okay, I had another problem to deal with. Should I call Helen and tell her that our kids were currently in the hands of a murderer?

All my instincts said no, absolutely not. Because Helen would certainly not sit in her hospital bed and wait for news.

She might demand that the police try to find her babies. She might hop into a wheelchair and look herself.

No, I couldn't tell her. It was too dangerous.

If Theresa and Kyle died, she'd hate me forever.

No she wouldn't. She would never hate me.

I didn't *think* she would.

Anyway, none of this mattered because the kids were going to be fine. One hundred percent fine.

I *had* to stop thinking about them! The riddle was the important thing right now!

"What the hell does it mean?" I said out loud, not caring if anyone overheard me.

By the time the taxi arrived, I still had no answer.

* * *

The library wasn't quite on the way home, but it was a small enough detour that I felt reasonably safe in asking the cabbie to drive by where I'd left my car. If it was still there, I'd have access to the physical clues instead of having to rely on my memory.

It had already been towed.

I told the cabbie to take me home.

* * *

When I got there I was surprised to find that Helen's car, now sporting a shattered windshield and a broken passenger-side window, was parked in the driveway. At first I thought Roger and the kids hadn't even gotten away from the house before they were jumped, but then I noticed that there was no safety glass on the pavement. The car had been driven back here. Theresa's bookbag wasn't inside, but the tape rested on the seat. The killer clearly didn't want me to be without my clue.

The first thing I did after I went inside was dial the number to Michael's cellular phone, hoping the killer would answer. He didn't.

I checked my watch. Eleven o'clock. One hour until I was supposed to be at the taping. One hour to either sit around the house and go absolutely positively totally freaking insane, or collect myself and try to figure out the clue.

The insane option sounded more appealing at the moment, but I forced myself to pop the tape back into the VCR, sit down on the couch, and watch the video again.

It was the same video, and my extra clues didn't provide any additional insights.

I leaned back, closed my eyes, and tried to relax. Maybe I was concentrating too hard. Maybe if I just lay there and let my thoughts flow freely, my subconscious might come up with something.

I tried that for about ten minutes. My subconscious didn't do squat.

I wondered if Theresa was sobbing now. Or screaming.

I watched the entire video yet again.

Nothing.

I paced around the house. Could the killer see me? Were Theresa and Kyle nearby?

And then it was eleven forty-five. Time to go.

* * *

Chamber doesn't have what you would call a slum, but the address was definitely in the poorest section of town. Didn't seem like the kind of area where the residents would have the extra income to pay to be the stars of their own horror movie.

I drove to the very end of the street, past some kids playing basketball using a hoop without netting, and into the driveway of a dilapidated two-story house that looked like it should be located next to an old graveyard at midnight.

There were no other cars in the driveway.

I checked to make sure I had the right address, and then got out of the car. Either everyone else was late, or there wasn't really a taping here.

Could everyone in Ghoulish Delights be in on it?

Or were none of them ever told to come here?

Nobody else had been around when Rachel gave me this address. It could have been a setup from the very beginning.

Well, I'd find out in short order.

I walked up to the front door and rung the doorbell. I didn't hear any buzzing or chiming from inside, so I figured it wasn't working. Not a big surprise. I knocked loudly, waited about thirty seconds, and then knocked again.

No answer. That wasn't a big surprise either.

I tried to peek through the windows, but the curtains

were drawn. I tested the doorknob. Unlocked.

Could Theresa and Kyle be in there? Could the killer have made it that easy?

I had to cancel that thought. Even if they were inside, I had a feeling that getting them back would be anything but easy.

I opened the door and stepped inside. If ever a house looked like a perfect site for a haunting, this was it. It had obviously been abandoned for quite some time, as there was a thick layer of dust over everything and cobwebs in every corner. Between the dust and the fading, I couldn't even tell what color the furniture was.

I took a step, and the floorboards creaked. I wondered if this is where I'd been tied to the chair. No, probably not...I hadn't noticed the thick musty scent before that I was smelling now. Even with the burlap sack over my head I should have been able to smell it.

The dust wasn't actually everywhere. A reasonably clean path ran from the doorway to the staircase, as if somebody had made several trips back and forth, enough to wipe away the dust and not so few as to leave individual footprints.

I could go ahead and explore the rest of the first floor, but it was pretty clear that if there was anything to find, I'd find it upstairs.

I flipped on the light switch, not really expecting it to work. I was correct. Even with the curtains closed, enough light streamed into the house that I could see where I was going, though upstairs would probably be a different story.

I began to ascend the stairs slowly, one at a time. They groaned with each step, but seemed sturdy and unlikely to collapse and send me plummeting into darkness beneath. A small pile of bones rested on the second-to-last step, possibly belonging to a bird.

At the top of the stairs, I turned left and found myself in a narrow hallway, with two doors on each side, and one door at the end. All of the doors were closed. There were no windows, and the light from downstairs provided only the faintest illumination. If only I'd known I'd be creeping around an abandoned house, I'd have brought a flashlight. I didn't even have Roger's lighter anymore. I could go buy one, I supposed, but there might not be much time. I'd have to make do with the little light available.

I slowly walked over to the first door on the right and opened it. The door made a horrible creak as it swung open, loud enough to awaken any slumbering ghosts. The room hadn't been entered in a long time. Dust covered the crib and the rattles on the floor.

I opened the door on the other side, wincing again at the creak. A bathroom. Vacant.

I continued down the hallway to the second set of doors. The first led to a bedroom. The mattress on the queen-sized bed had been torn apart, with stuffing flung everywhere. I couldn't see well enough to tell if the dust had been disturbed or not.

"Hello?" I called out.

No answer.

I listened carefully for a few moments. Total silence. Nobody was here.

I opened the opposite door, which also led to a bedroom. Once again, I listened and heard nothing.

Theresa and Kyle could be underneath the bed, blood pooling beneath their bodies as spiders scurry over their faces...

I almost had to hit myself to break the thought process. I turned to the door at the end of the hallway and opened it.

No creak.

It opened to a closet. Empty, except for a ladder leading up to the attic.

I stepped into the closet and looked up. No light at all.

I had to get a flashlight. Borrow one from a neighbor or something.

"Hello?" I called out. "Is anyone up there?"

Nobody responded.

"Theresa! Kyle! Are you there?"

Something in the attic rattled.

Then I thought I heard something else. Maybe a voice, but faint and muffled.

Screw the flashlight. I was going up there *now*.

I gripped the ladder tightly and began to climb. It held my weight fine, and I made it to the top without breaking any bones. The attic was completely dark, except for a tiny bit of light streaming in from underneath some curtains. The window was only a couple of steps away from the ladder, so I carefully put my foot down on the attic floor. It seemed like it would hold me. I walked the two paces to the window, and pulled the curtains, filling the attic with light.

It wasn't difficult to figure out what I was here to find.

The attic looked like a zoo hitting hard times, loaded with cages but not enough animals to fill them. There were at least a dozen cages up here, but only four of them were occupied. And the inhabitants of these cages weren't animals—they were people. None of them were Theresa or Kyle.

Bound and wrist and ankle by thick chains, the four prisoners suffered in cages barely large enough for a human. The captives seemed to be in their street clothes, except that their heads were completely covered with black leather masks, as if they were executioners who found themselves on the wrong side of the chopping block. The masks had openings over the nose, but no eye holes, and only a closed zipper over the mouth.

I took a step forward. "Can you hear me?" I asked in a loud voice.

There was an immediate reaction of writhing and muffled groans. I knelt down next to the first cage, which held a dangerously thin woman whose blouse was covered with dirt and mostly unbuttoned. I rattled the door of the cage, but a padlock held it shut. There were padlocks around her chains as well. Fortunately, the bars of the cage were far enough apart that I could squeeze my hand through. I put my hand on her shoulder, and the woman flinched as if my hand was an ice pick jabbing into her flesh.

"It's okay," I whispered. "I'm here to help."

A zipper ran up the back of her mask. I twisted my arm into a good position, and then slowly, so as not to startle her, I unzipped it all the way and slid the mask off her face. The zipper caught on her tangled, dirty blonde hair, but I removed it gently and let the mask fall to the floor.

The woman squinted and let out a whimper as the light struck her eyes. There was an ugly bruise on her chin, but otherwise she seemed physically unharmed.

"Who are you?" she asked.

"My name is Andrew Mayhem. I'm going to get you out of here, I promise. But I need your help. Do you know who did this to you?"

She shook her head. "There was more than one. I never saw any of them." Her voice grew frantic. "Please, you have to get me out of this place before they come back! They've come and taken away most of the others already! Please! I can't stand it anymore!"

"I need you to calm down for me," I said, not raising my voice. "What's your name?"

"Tracy."

"Tracy, you'll be free before you know it. Now, what about the keys? Do you have any idea where they are?"

She shook her head rapidly.

"How long have you been here?"

"I don't know...days...weeks...the mask never comes off. It was so hard to breathe. I thought I was going to die. They take us out of the cages sometimes, once a day, I don't know, and let us walk around for a few minutes. They shove some food down our throats, give us some water, yank down our pants and shove us on a bedpan, but then we're locked up again."

"Would you recognize any of the voices?" I asked.

"No. They never talk in front of us."

"Okay, look, I don't have anything to cut the padlocks with, but I'm going to..."

I stopped in mid-sentence as I looked across the attic and saw a wood-chopping axe lying on the floor. Either a forgetful lumberjack had been in the vicinity, or that was what I was meant to use.

It seemed a little too easy. The killer had to have a surprise waiting.

But I certainly couldn't leave these people here, so I made my way across the attic and retrieved the axe. It was a nice, solid tool, which I was happy to note was not covered with blood. I stopped at the nearest cage, which held a man who sat pressed against the corner.

"I'm not going to hurt you," I said. "I'm going to take that mask off, then I'm going to set you free."

The man nodded. I reached inside, unzipped the mask from the back, and pulled it off him. The man's face was a bruised and bloody mess. I wondered if he'd put up a struggle when he was kidnapped, or if they'd done it afterward.

"Thank you," he whispered.

I removed the masks of the other two people. Their faces were in about the same condition as Tracy's—a bruise or two, but nothing serious. All four of them were from the coming attractions segment of the first video.

I returned to Tracy's cage, lifted the axe, then brought it down as hard as I could upon the padlock on the cage door. The cage shook with a loud clatter, but the padlock remained in place. With the second swing, however, the padlock dropped to the ground and I pulled the door open.

The locks on the chains were going to be more difficult because I could only raise the axe as far as the top of the cage. And since they were right next to Tracy's ankles and wrists, there was always the chance of a nasty accident.

"Don't move," I told her.

"I couldn't if I wanted to," she said.

I slammed the axe down on the padlock binding her ankles, but it didn't break. I was too concerned about accidentally chopping off one of Tracy's feet to hit it with full force. In theory, much worse things than losing a foot would happen if I didn't get the prisoners out of here in time, but I couldn't help trying to be careful.

"Andrew?"

I froze at the sound of the voice.

"Andrew, are you here? It's me, Rachel!"

For a few seconds I allowed myself to feel relief that I now had somebody to help me free the prisoners, but that was soon replaced with a sense of unease. After all, who had given me the location of the "taping" in the first place? Very possibly, I'd put my trust in the wrong person.

"C'mon, Andrew, I know you're here! I saw your car out front!" How would she recognize Helen's car? I cautiously stepped away from Tracy's cage, still holding the axe.

"Andrew, talk to me! Are you here or what?"

Her voice was closer. She was on the second floor now.

There was silence for almost a full minute except for Rachel's footsteps. I eased my way over to the ladder, gripping the axe handle tightly with both hands, making sure I couldn't be seen from below. Then a flashlight beam shone on the ceiling.

"What, are you hiding up in the attic? C'mon, I'm not gonna hurt you, for God's sake!"

They'd done well so far, and I prayed the prisoners would continue to remain silent.

"Okay, I'm coming up. Don't shoot me or anything, please."

The ladder creaked as Rachel began to climb. I stood by the entrance, just out of sight, axe poised and ready to strike.

CHAPTER
TWENTY
ONE

Rachel's left hand came into view, and then her right hand, which was holding the flashlight as well as gripping the ladder. Then her head rose up above the entrance. Her eyes widened as she saw me holding the axe. "Whoa! Settle!"

"What do you want?" I demanded.

"Could you maybe put the axe down?"

"I could, but I'm choosing not to."

"Fine, but could you promise not to hit me with it as long as I don't make any sudden moves?"

"Sure."

"Can I come up?"

"I'd rather you didn't."

"Suit yourself." She glanced over her shoulder and for the first time noticed the prisoners in the cages. "Oh my God..." she gasped. "Are these the people you were telling me about? Sorry, dumb question, but Andrew, we've got to get them out of here!"

"That was my plan."

Rachel sighed. "Okay, look, it's pretty obvious what you're thinking. But listen to me, Andrew—I had nothing to do with this! Nothing! And every second you waste not believing me is time that we should be using to set these people free!"

"Why did you come here?" I asked.

"To check the place out before the taping. Nobody lives

here, so I figured I could look around beforehand."

"Uh-huh. And how did you know it was my car?"

"There were toys in the backseat. Nobody in Ghoulish Delights has kids, and it certainly wasn't out of the question that you'd show up here, so I took a guess. C'mon, Andrew, let's not risk the lives of these people just because you're being paranoid."

"Okay," I said, stepping back as my stomach tightened at the mention of my kids. "You can come up."

She climbed all the way into the attic. "So what's the situation?"

"They're chained to the floor and I don't have the key. I'm going to have to use the axe to break them free."

"Why don't you let me try it?"

"Thanks, but no."

"Oh, for God's sake, Andrew, are you saying you can't trust me with the axe?"

"At this point I'm not really up to trusting anyone."

"Goddammit!" shouted Tracy from her cage. "Give her the fucking axe so we can get out of here!"

"Nobody asked your opinion," I informed her.

"Okay, how about this?" Rachel pointed to the far end of the attic. "You walk over there and set the axe on one of the cages, then you climb down the ladder to safety. That way I won't have a chance to chop your head off before I start bashing padlocks."

I stared at her for a long moment. "Ah, screw it," I said, and handed her the axe.

"Thank you." Rachel tested the axe's weight with both hands as she walked over to Tracy's cage. "I could have taken this from you in about two seconds, but I wanted to give you a chance to cooperate nicely."

"If you say so."

"Don't move," Rachel told Tracy. She took a practice swing in slow motion to make sure the axe was positioned correctly, then brought it down hard, breaking the lock that held her ankles.

"Oh, God, thank you!" said Tracy, as Rachel positioned the axe to break the lock binding her wrists.

"So did I miss any other developments?" asked Rachel.

"The killer has my children."

"*What?*"

She finished setting Tracy free, and I told her everything that happened since we'd last met. Tracy could barely walk, so I helped her move around the floor, working her arms and legs to get the blood flowing again. By the time I'd finished the story, two more prisoners were free, leaving only the man with the battered face.

"One after the creation of the other," muttered Rachel. "What could that possibly mean?"

"I have no idea," I admitted.

"What kind of condom was it?"

"Trojan, I think. Trojan after the creation of the mail. Mail after the creation of the Trojan." I shrugged. "Doesn't help."

Or did it? What did the Trojans create? I only remembered about .007% of what I'd learned in history class, but I did recall the story of the Trojan horse.

"Something after the horse?" I said aloud. "Can you think of anyplace a horse might be important?"

Rachel thought for a moment. "Not off the top of my head, not here in Chamber."

"Wouldn't letters be more appropriate than mail?" inquired Tracy, massaging her ankles.

"Letters after the horse," I said. "Specifically, five letters after the horse. The fifth letter would be 'E.' What could that mean?" Nothing sprung to mind. "Or maybe it's like one of those codes we used to do in grade school, where B means A, and C means B, and so on. That would make it...I, J, K, L, M for the first letter, giving us Morse, and then—"

I stopped as I had a sudden realization. That's why the skull's movement seemed so weird! "The skull is speaking in Morse code!"

"Are you sure?" asked Rachel.

"That has to be it! That's the answer!" My heart was pounding so quickly I thought it was ready to break out of my chest and onto the dirty floor. "I have to go somewhere I can look at the tape!"

"Go, then!" said Rachel, lifting the axe to break through the last of the man's locks. "I'll get everyone out of here and take them to the police."

"No, you can't do that yet," I said. Rachel smashed through the padlock and began to help the man out of his cage. "Take them somewhere safe, hidden away. Put them in your car and just drive out of Chamber, get as far away as you can. Give me until midnight to take care of everything, then go to the police."

Rachel nodded as she turned to the former prisoners. "Any objections to giving our friend a chance to get his kids back?"

They all shook their heads.

"Then get out of here," Rachel told me. "I'll see you later."

* * *

My jubilation at solving the riddle was tainted by a sick feeling that things were going to get a whole lot uglier before they got better. Because really, the killer had just handed the prisoners over to us. No challenge. Which meant that he had something much worse in store.

There was no way in hell I was going to speed after the results of my last little traffic violation, so I kept to the posted limit until I saw both of what I needed in a strip mall to my right. Pages-A-Plenty and Chamber Video World.

I hurried into the small bookstore and pushed past a young woman who was at the front counter with a stack of self-help books. "Sorry," I said to the cashier, "but this is life or death. I need a book on Morse code."

The cashier was a tall gentleman with wire framed glasses and hair that was gray at the temples. "I believe that you should wait your turn."

"Listen to me," I said, leaning forward. "Direct me to a book on Morse code or your potential customers are going to be frightened away by me doing a naked limbo in your front window."

"Books on Amateur Radio should be in the hobby section, back wall, middle shelf," said the cashier, quickly.

"Thanks. By the way, could I borrow a pen?"

The cashier handed me a pen. "Keep it."

I hurried to the back shelf and searched for a moment until I located *Amateur Radio Made Easy*. I flipped through the pages and found one that listed all of the letters and their Morse code dot-dash equivalents. I didn't have any money and I figured that stealing a book wasn't the best course of action to take when police involvement is considered bad, so

I scribbled the code down on my arm and left the store.

I proceeded to the movie rental place. A monitor above the checkout counter was playing that stupid *Zany the Chipper Chipmunk* video. There were only a couple of customers wandering the aisles (no doubt due to Zany's evil presence) and a teenage girl behind the counter.

"Hi," I said to her, setting the Ghoulish Delights tape on the counter. "I'm a private investigator for the state, and I need to commandeer your VCR."

"Huh?" replied the girl.

"I need you to play this tape for me."

"I can't do that. The manager tells us what movies to play."

"Is the manager around now?"

The girl shook her head.

"Then let's not worry about him. Play this. Actually, let me play it...I'm going to need to do a lot of rewinding." I stepped behind the counter and ejected Zany from the VCR.

"Sir, customers aren't allowed behind the counter," the girl insisted.

"I'm not a customer. I have no intention of renting anything." I inserted the Ghoulish Delights tape into the VCR and pressed play. "Can you mute the volume?" I asked. "I don't want the voices to distract me."

The girl nodded, picked up another remote, and shut off the sound. As the talking skulls came on, I focused all of my attention on Boo-Boo. Yes, his mouth was definitely moving in a series of long and short beats, with pauses that hopefully signaled a space between letters.

I rewound to the beginning of Boo-Boo's dialogue, and wrote down what I saw.

Quick bite, quick bite, pause, quick bite, slow bite, pause...

I lost the flow, rewound, and started again, confirming what I'd written and then picking up where I'd left off.

Slow bite, pause, quick bite, quick bite, quick bite, quick bite, pause, quick bite...

Dash, dash, pause, dot, dot, pause, dash, dash, dot...

"What movie is that?" asked one of the customers. "My son would probably enjoy that kind of garbage."

I ignored him. It took more than ten rewinds to get the entire message, but soon I had everything written down on my arm. Comparing my left arm to my right, I began to translate the message.

I AM THE MIGHTY HUNTER. COME AND GET ME.

It was Mr. Dead Fish Cologne himself. Dominick!

* * *

"Oh, hi Andrew, how's the search go—HEY!!!"

Linda cried out as I wrapped my arm around her neck and pressed the edge of the K-Mart kitchen knife against her throat. I pushed my way into the living room of the apartment and kicked the door shut behind me. "Is Dominick home?" I asked in a whisper.

"Yes."

"Call him out here."

"Dominick, honey, Andrew's here to see you!"

Dominick stepped into the room, a half-eaten Pop-Tart in one hand. "Oh, hi, Andy. Welcome to my humble home. Do you want the tour before or after you decapitate my girlfriend?"

"Where the hell are my kids?" I demanded.

Dominick shrugged. "I'm not sure. Probably the same place I stashed Michael." He grinned and took another bite of his Pop-Tart. "By the way, Linda, if Andrew doesn't end up killing you, please remember to get the frosted kind next time."

"I'll try, sweetheart," Linda said.

"Tell me where my kids are or I'll cut her!" I threatened. "I mean it! This isn't a joke!"

"Oh, that's right, I'm supposed to be taking this all very seriously," said Dominick. "Please forgive me, I have a tendency to behave inappropriately in certain social situations. So, let me get this straight, you want me to return your kids to you in exchange for Linda's life, correct?"

"That's the idea."

"And what makes you think I care if Linda lives or dies? Sure, she has some really cute dimples and a fantastic ass, but her personality is just loaded with defects."

I removed the knife from Linda's throat, and then poked the tip into the side of her neck. She cried out in pain as blood welled from the tiny wound.

"Hey, what the hell are you doing?" shouted Dominick, his eyes wide.

"I'm not kidding around here! Give me back my kids!"

Then I let out my own cry of pain as Linda stomped on my toes with her heel. It didn't hurt enough to make me drop my knife, but her next move, jabbing her elbow into my gut, was enough to double me over. Great. I'd seen a dozen movies where the woman escaped her captor by stomping his foot, and now it happened to me in real life. Real smooth.

I stood back up and grabbed her hair. Though she didn't have long, flowing tresses, I was able to get a good handful and yank her toward me. This time I pressed the knife against the back of her neck, and she froze.

Dominick was gone.

"Get out here!" I shouted. "I swear to God, Dominick, you don't want to mess with somebody as screwed up as I am right now!"

Dominick stepped back into the living room, now holding a crossbow pointed in my direction. I had Linda in front of me as a shield, but she didn't cover me completely. Hopefully his aim wasn't perfect.

"Drop the crossbow or I'll stab her," I said.

"You stab her and you get an arrow through the face," Dominick said. "Then your kids will die."

"Where are they?" I demanded.

"I don't know. I didn't touch them."

"Bullshit, oh mighty hunter."

"I have no idea what you're talking about. All I know is that this was supposed to be a joke."

"It's no joke," I said. "My children have been kidnapped."

"By who?"

"Well, obviously I thought it was by you! Who told you this was a joke?"

"I was talking to Carl this morning. He said that you weren't a detective, you were somebody Michael hired as a practical joke and that we were supposed to play along."

"I think it's a pretty big understatement to say that you were severely misinformed."

"I consider myself informed now. Why don't you let her go so we can talk this over?"

I shook my head. "You put down the crossbow first."

Dominick bent down at the knees and carefully set the crossbow down on the floor. He stood up and held up his hands to show that they were empty.

"Kick it over here," I said.

Dominick hesitated. "This bow was really expensive."

"Now!"

He kicked the bow. It slid across the floor, coming to a stop about two feet from me. I removed the knife from Linda's neck and she hurried over to Dominick. "Asshole!" she said, slapping him across the chest. "Don't you *ever* worry about how much your precious bow is worth when some maniac is attacking me with a knife!"

I wondered if this was the way I was going to solve the mystery, by threatening each of the potential suspects with sharp objects until one of them turned out to be the killer.

"So what brings you here?" asked Dominick.

"Some psycho has me running all over the place playing his game," I said. "The final clue was I AM THE MIGHTY HUNTER. That would be you, right?"

"Well, no, not really, I just fish," Dominick explained. "I have a huge weapon collection, but it's not used for hunting. I swear, I have nothing to do with whatever it is you're involved in." He turned to Linda. "Do you have any idea what he's talking about?"

"The son of a bitch is crazy," said Linda. "He probably murdered his kids himself."

"*I'm not crazy!*" I shouted, furious. I took a deep breath to calm myself down. "Okay, maybe I am a little, but I'm not lying about this. If Dominick isn't the mighty hunter, who is?"

Linda avoided my gaze.

Then a possibility occurred to me. The game—Prophecies of the Night.

"In Prophecies of the Night, is one of the character types a hunter?" I asked.

Dominick shrugged and glanced at Linda. "I'm not sure," she said. "There are so many I'd think there would have to be."

I tried to remember what I'd heard from the game. I stood there, concentrating, trying to recall any piece of conversation that indicated who might play a hunter.

A flash of dialogue ran through my mind.

"...I'll add his head to my trophy case..."

"It's Farley!" I exclaimed. "The mighty hunter is Farley!

He has my kids!"

I turned and started to bolt for the door. "Hold on, wait a second!" said Dominick. "Should we call the police?"

"No police! That's the recurring theme of Farley's threats! I have to go after him myself!"

"Okay, we don't need to involve the cops, but I'll come with you!"

"You're not going anywhere!" Linda protested. "The guy is insane, can't you tell?"

Dominick shook his head. "There's always been something about Farley that creeped me out. I have no problem at all believing that he's a kidnapper."

"And a murderer," I said. "He buried Michael alive and chopped up Jennifer."

"Jennifer's dead?" Dominick took a few seconds to digest that information then continued. "Okay, if what you say about Farley is true, then you can't just confront him with a kitchen knife. But you may also be completely wrong, so I'm not sending you after him without supervision. I mean, you could've really hurt Linda and she had nothing to do with this."

"I don't need supervision," I said.

"I think you do. And if you take me along, I can arm you to the teeth. I've got an incredible collection of weapons in the other room, not all of them legal, if you get my drift."

"Well then, why don't you tag along?" I suggested.

"Good idea. Let's go get some *stuff.*"

CHAPTER TWENTY TWO

There were no cars in the driveway as we pulled up alongside Farley's home. It was a fairly nice place, if a bit small. Personally, I would've figured Farley to be the kind of guy who still lived with his parents.

The three of us got out of Helen's car. I'd told them the whole story on the way, to make sure they understood just how dangerous things could be. Linda had refused to let Dominick go without her, and all three of us were wielding crossbows. I also had a belt from which dangled two vicious-looking knives, and a quiver containing a combination of about twenty arrows and bolts, everything from one with an explosive tip to a razor-lined one that I was supposed to handle very, very carefully.

After we each placed a bolt into our crossbows and pulled them back, locked into place and ready to fire, we walked up to the front door and I knocked. "Farley, it's me," I called out.

No answer.

"I know that you're the mighty hunter," I said. "Open the door and let's talk."

Still nothing. I tested the doorknob and found it unlocked. "You guys ready?" I asked.

Dominick nodded. Linda shook her head.

I turned the knob and pushed the door open. "Come on out, Farley!" I shouted into the darkness. I reached inside and flipped on the light switch. The living room looked a lot like the Ghoulish Delights office—a shrine to horror movies. The walls were covered with posters, and all sorts of masks, models, creatures, and other assorted morbid props were carefully placed for maximum gruesome impact. More interesting were the six or seven cables that stretched across the room just inches below the ceiling, one end of each fastened to the wall at our right, the other end disappearing into a hallway.

"Theresa?" I called out. "Kyle? Can you hear me?"

No response, not that I expected one.

Then I saw Boo-Boo. The skull was at the far end of the room, resting on top of a television set, an envelope in his mouth.

"I need to get that envelope," I said, pointing. "You two stay put. Cover me."

Dominick and Linda raised their crossbows in a position to best shoot any assailant. I moved my own slowly, from side to side, and then began to move forward. The first cable was only a couple of feet away.

Three steps later there was a loud squeaking sound, and then suddenly a corpse burst out of the hallway, hanging from a pulley attached to the cable. At least a dozen blades protruded from the body, and I barely jumped back in time to avoid being sliced. The corpse slammed against the wall and dangled there, bouncing and swaying like a flesh-and-blood puppet.

It was a man, and he'd been completely dismembered. The pieces were now held together with wire, with inch-long gaps in between each chunk. Except for the head, which hung a good six inches above the rest of the body.

I turned around. Dominick and Linda both looked ready to keel over, but neither of them screamed.

"I won't be offended if you want to wait in the car."

"Just get the fucking envelope!" Dominick snapped.

From this angle, I still couldn't see into the hallway. The toes of the corpse dangled about a foot above the floor, so it would be too dangerous to try to crawl over to the envelope if another body shot out. I took another step forward, then another, and then leapt back as I heard a second series of squeaks.

Another corpse burst out of the hallway. This time dodging was unnecessary, because the wire snapped and the body dropped in a heap on the floor. Only the head, adorned with several fishhooks, slammed against the wall.

Okay, I was wasting time. I braced myself, and then ran at top speed across the room. Out of the corner of my eye I saw four corpses shoot out of the hallway, one after the other. I reached Boo-Boo and snatched the envelope out of his mouth as the corpses bashed into the wall.

I looked at them. All had various weapons protruding from them, from a long spear to a non-running chainsaw. Two of the corpses hadn't been reconstructed properly, their body parts switched around in some appalling mix-and-match game.

"Welcome to the mind of Farley," I said. Dominick and Linda had nothing to say to that.

I opened the envelope, which was labeled "For Andrew" and read the note inside.

"Congratulations, Andrew! You've done great! Okay, I can't say that for sure—it may have taken you too long to find this, and I may have slaughtered your kiddies out of boredom. But for now let's pretend I haven't. It's time for the moment you've been waiting for. The final showdown. The big explanation. Fun, fun, fun for the whole family! Can you handle this much excitement??? Follow the enclosed map and see what happens! As usual, do it alone or I'll kill your kids, yadda yadda yadda. This time I mean it. Your very bestest friend in the whole wide world, Farley."

So really, Farley set things up so that I hadn't ever needed to solve that Morse-code-condom riddle. I could've just broken one of his precious rules and showed up at his house early. What a dickhead.

"What does it say?" asked Dominick.

I looked at the hand-drawn map. It was directions to a cabin, located not too far from the park where I'd dug up Michael in the first place. Probably the cabin where I'd been tied up and listened to Jennifer meet her demise.

"It tells where he is," I told him. "And I have to go alone."

"I'm sorry to hear that," said Linda, not removing her gaze from the corpses.

"Watch yourselves," I said. "I'm heading back."

I ran across the room, expecting more corpses to come flying at me, but apparently they'd all been used in the first round. We left the house, closing the door behind us to keep any nosy neighbors from peeking inside. I really didn't need anyone else dropping dead of a heart attack this week.

"Is there anything else I can do?" asked Dominick.

I considered saying, "You can pray." But that seemed a little too melodramatic. So I said something that was more in tune with my personality.

"Sure, you can reshingle my roof while I'm off saving my kids. I've got Popsicles in the freezer for when you take a break."

Dominick didn't smile. "Seriously, I hope things work out for you."

"So do I."

* * *

Farley may have been an annoying psychopathic little geek, but he did know how to draw a map. This meant less time that I had to drive around lost, and thus less time for me to envision Theresa and Kyle hanging from a cable, their heads switched around and not quite connected with their necks.

About six miles after driving past Fleet Park, I reached the unnamed road marked on the map. It took another three miles before I reached the windowless cabin, which looked barely able to sustain its own weight. Firewood was stacked by the door, and a white Chevrolet was parked in the driveway. A bumper sticker read "Grandma Went To Hell And All I Got Was This Lousy Bumper Sticker."

I parked Helen's car, got out, adjusted the quiver on my back, and slowly approached the door.

"Come on in!" Farley called from inside.

I pulled the door open.

"Before you try anything, make sure you take a good look at the setup here," he warned.

I stepped inside the cabin, crossbow ready to fire. Farley stood near the far wall, about twenty feet away. Theresa and Kyle stood next to him, one on each side, their faces tearstained. I was overjoyed to see that they were still alive, but that joy vanished as I realized just how bad the situation really was.

Farley held a brick in each hand with a wire wrapped around it. The wires stretched up to the ceiling, looped around a pair of hooks, then continued down to form something like necklaces for Theresa and Kyle. Necklaces lined with dozens upon dozens of razor blades.

"See what we've got here?" asked Farley, lowering one of the bricks slightly. Theresa's necklace tightened just a bit and she let out a soft whimper. "I drop these bricks, and your kids get shredded throats. So I'd say it's in your best interest not to make me drop the bricks. You can go ahead and shoot me if you'd like, but things will turn out very messy."

I set the crossbow down on the floor. "I won't do anything," I said.

"Good boy." Farley looked at Kyle and grinned. "Your daddy likes you. You should feel happy."

Kyle, frozen with terror, didn't say anything.

"I hope you were a smart guy, Andrew," said Farley. "If you brought any cops or other friends and I see them, these bricks are gonna fall. If you hired a sniper or something, you may want to call him off before he gets an itchy trigger finger."

"I'm alone," I said.

"Good. So we can talk. Care for a seat? Your kids and I can't sit down for obvious reasons, but that's no reason why you shouldn't be comfortable."

"I'll stand."

"Suit yourself. So I guess the big question is, why have I called you here? What's the meaning of all this nonsense with the riddles and the dismembered pieces of Jennifer in your friend's car and the charming videos and, oh, everything you've had to go through these past couple of days. Well, you're in luck. Here's where I explain everything."

I noticed that Theresa's leg was starting to wobble. "She's not going to be able to stand like that much longer," I said. "Let my kids go. You can take all my weapons. I won't be able to try anything."

Farley shook his head. "She'll be okay, we just got into place a few minutes ago, after you set off the sensors. But I'm going to let you in on a cruel little secret. Your kids are history. Whatever happens, I'll eventually have to drop these bricks, and the razor blades will do what they do best. It's gonna be bloody, believe me. You can beg, you can plead, you can bribe, you can threaten, you can do whatever you want, but in the end the bricks are going to fall. So really, you might as well just pick up that crossbow and take me down right now. But you won't do that, because you're going to be searching for a way out of this. Which means I get to talk."

I noticed a video camera on a tripod in the corner of the cabin. The red light was flashing. "Recording this for posterity?" I asked.

"Yep. This'll help you out in tying up any loose ends with the police, and this way you won't have to take notes. So, look around you, Andrew, because this is where the magic happens."

I glanced around the cabin. There were numerous bloodstains on the floor, and I recognized the bed from the videos. Various implements of torture were hung on the walls. A small shelf against the far wall contained videotapes, more weapons, and Gaggles, still wearing his cowboy hat.

"Yeah, this is where we brought the victims. I didn't have anything to do with the actual kidnappings—that was the work of The Apparition and a couple other folks, but once they were here and the cameras were ready to roll...ooohhh, baby, we had some good times. I was the guy who did the actual killings. Remember the spork? Good work, huh?"

"Sure, high quality all around," I muttered.

Farley was right...I was desperately trying to figure out a way out of this, but what could I do? Any action I took against him would make him drop the bricks, and then Theresa and Kyle would die. I could try to rush him, but was there any way to reach him before he let the bricks fall? I didn't stand a chance.

"Anyway, that's where the real money for Ghoulish Delights came from. We'd been socking it away, having ourselves a great time while we tried to save up enough to retire somewhere."

"Who's we?" I asked.

"Me, Michael, and Jennifer. Your buddies Rachel, Dominick, Linda, and Carl were all blissfully unaware of the *real* Ghoulish Delights. They probably would have been offended by the idea. Some people are so conservative."

Theresa's leg was wobbling even more. I wanted more than anything to hurry over to her, but that would kill her.

"So, everything was going fine, until one dark night when Jennifer was snooping around in Michael's computer. And what did she discover but that her dear husband, who was in charge of all the client contact for our made-to-order snuff videos, had been hiding away a lot of money that he never told her about. Where's the sense of trust in marriage these days? So she confronted him, they fought, she stormed off, and then she came over to my place to tell me what he'd done. She was in a vengeful mood and I had nothing against the idea of getting laid for revenge, so we went at it until Michael showed up at my door. I'm sorry, is this story inappropriate for children?"

"A story involving you having sex is inappropriate for anyone without a cast-iron stomach," I said.

"Ooohhh, good slam for Andrew! Anyway, Michael was all bent out of shape and he threatened to turn us all in. Jennifer managed to calm him down, we all apologized, and Jennifer and Michael decided they needed some time alone, to work things out. So they set up a trip to Europe. Are you sure you don't want to sit down?"

"I'm fine."

"But Jennifer, of course, never intended to go to Europe. We decided we were going to kill her scumbag husband in the worst way possible. So, Tuesday night, I threw an unassembled pine coffin into the trunk of my car, forced Michael from his home at gunpoint, and drove him out to Fleet Park. I made him dig his own hole, construct his own coffin, then lie down in it. Stretched the whole thing out as much as I could—a total blast. But then he started begging for mercy. I mean, *begging*. It would've broken your heart. I don't know what happened to me, I just felt sorry for the poor guy. So I knocked him out with chloroform and tossed the gun in the coffin before I locked it shut and reburied it. That way, you know, if things were too unbearable he could always kill himself. I regretted it later, I mean, what a wuss thing to do, but don't say I never did anything nice for anyone."

"Does this mean if I start begging you'll let my kids go?"

Farley shook his head. "Nah, I'll just drop the brick sooner.

Anyway, that should've fixed all our problems, but then we realized we didn't know where the key to his safe was. We tore the place apart, and no key. Finally we decided he had it on him."

"That sounds like something you should have thought about before you buried him," I remarked.

"Yeah, well, I never claimed to be a criminal genius. Then the next night that bitch Jennifer decided to go behind my back and hire you to dig up the coffin. Really stupid on her part, but I guess the idea of digging him up herself freaked her out. So I followed her, and really you should be grateful because I ended up saving your life. She planned to kill both of you after you found the key, but my little rampage put a stop to that. So I brought all three of you back here...I'm stronger than I look, by the way...hacked up Jennifer, and figured I'd use Roger as a hostage until I got the money.

"But then everything turned to shit. I opened the safe, nearly got shot by a poisoned dart, and discovered that the only thing in the safe was a friendly little note. I don't know who was holding the evidence against us, but if Michael didn't get in touch with him by Friday night, tonight, everything was going straight to the FBI. Michael had babbled something about this while I was burying him alive, but I thought it was just a trick to save his life. I realized that I was, in a word, fucked."

"Not a great feeling, is it?" I asked.

"Ah, it's not so bad once you get over it. And that's when I decided, to hell with it. I'm not living my life as a fugitive, and I'm certainly not going to prison. I've had a pretty wild life, killed a lot of people. I figured it was time to, as the quote goes, die young and leave a beautiful corpse. But I wanted people to know who I was, what I'd done. I wanted to be famous like Jeffrey Dahmer, Son of Sam, Ted Bundy, all of those guys. So that's where you came in."

Theresa's leg was now wobbling so violently that I thought she was going to drop at any second. But what could I do? I clenched my fists and gritted my teeth and forced myself not to lunge forward.

"You were already involved," Farley explained, "so I figured I'd make you my personal spokesperson. I'd put you through an outrageous hell, give you the story of a lifetime, even let you be the one to kill me. I have to say—you did incredibly well. I did hide multiple clues at the graveyard to increase your chances, but still...kudos to you. And I got to reuse my favorite prop, the Dismemberment Game I built for a very special episode of Ghoulish Delights. The questions are really easy to program. I'll let you keep it if you want."

"No thanks."

"Anyway, I figured I'd turn your life into an absolutely crazy nightmare, and then my fame would be guaranteed, as would yours. You'd even get the better end of the deal. After all, I'll be dead, and all you'll have done is lose your children."

"You don't have to kill them," I insisted. "You want fame? I've gone through enough freaky shit in the past couple days to guarantee you a spot in the Psychopath Hall of Fame."

"I know, but it's just too good to pass up. Hear the story of Farley Soukup from the guy who watched his own children die."

"I swear, if you hurt them I won't say a goddamn word."

"Uh-huh. Yeah, right. What're you going to do, bury all the evidence? Hide the bodies of your children and pretend a wild dingo carried them off?"

Farley turned his wrist slightly, checking his watch. "You know, these bricks are starting to get a bit heavy. If you have any final dramatic statement to make, now's the time. Say goodbye to your kids, Andrew. Make it good. The camera's rolling."

CHAPTER TWENTY THREE

"You want this to be a game, right?" I asked. "Then give me a chance to try and set them free."

"You have plenty of chances," said Farley. "It's just that none of them will work."

I reached down and picked up the crossbow. "Give me two shots. One for each wire."

"You're going to snap the wire with an arrow?" Farley asked, tremendously amused.

"I'm gonna try."

"Oh, well, don't let me stop you! Hell, if you're that good of a shot you deserve your kids back! But you stay where you are. Come any closer and I drop the bricks."

"I understand." I held up the crossbow and peered through the sight, aiming it at the wire that connected to Theresa's razor blade necklace.

"I think there might be an apple somewhere around here, if you want to put it on her head," said Farley.

I ignored him, kept my arm as steady as possible, and pulled the trigger.

The bolt shot past the wire, missing it by about six inches. Better than I would've expected.

"Good shot!" said Farley. "Not good enough, but I'm still impressed. I would applaud, but I don't think you'd appreciate that. Oh well, I guess this means the girl's dead. Wanna try to save the boy?"

I took an arrow out of the quiver, pulled back the bow-string, and locked it in place. Then I took careful aim at Theresa's wire again.

"Oh, trying for the girl again, huh? I don't blame you. She's older, you've got more of an investment in her."

I placed my finger on the trigger, took a deep breath, and shot the arrow.

But not at the wire. At the last instant I jerked the cross-bow upward, firing at the hook. The explosive-tipped arrow I'd gotten from Dominick hit the ceiling, creating a monstrous ball of fire and sending chunks of wood flying everywhere.

The noise was deafening. Farley dropped the bricks as he was thrown to the ground, and the hooks and wires fell with them, along with half of the roof.

I staggered backwards from the impact, accidentally drop-ping the crossbow, then immediately hurried forward. "Theresa! Kyle! Get out of here!" I screamed, shoving them toward the doorway. The kids rushed for safety, as Farley made a lunge to grab the wire that trailed behind Kyle.

I kicked Farley in the face before he could manage that. He rolled on his side as some burning wood pieces fell on his leg. I tried to kick him again, but he moved out of the way in time. He grabbed a piece of rubble and threw it at me, graz-ing my shoulder and instantly causing my arm to go numb. Then he got to his feet.

"Your kids are still gonna die!" he shouted. "You haven't changed anything!"

He rushed at me like a football player going for a tackle. As I dodged, I realized my mistake—Farley snatched the cross-bow and a razor-lined arrow from the floor. I ran toward him, whipping an arrow from my own quiver.

He swung the crossbow, bashing me in the temple. I stumbled backward several steps and fell on a burning chunk of the ceiling. I cried out and rolled over, frantically batting at my shirt. As I beat out the flames, Farley snapped the arrow into place.

He fired. The arrow struck me, sinking half its length into my upper arm, jutting out the other side. I couldn't even scream—I could only let out a series of frantic gasps.

Although the pain was so intense that I wanted nothing

more than to just curl up into a little ball and cry, I forced myself to stand up again as Farley picked up another arrow and prepared to fire. This time he shot it into my right leg, inches below the waist. I fell back and crashed into the shelf in an explosion of videos and weapons.

Farley tossed the crossbow down and glared at me. He walked over to a small dresser beside the bed and opened one of the drawers. "You're lucky I didn't put the arrow through your eye," he said, taking out a handgun. "But I still want you to live."

He strode toward the doorway. "What do I do now, huh? I guess I hunt down your brats, put a bullet in each of them, and then wait for the cops to show up to investigate the explosion. I can go down in a hail of bullets like Bonnie and Clyde. Not as good as my original plan, but what can you do?"

I moaned and tried to push myself to a sitting position. Farley rolled his eyes and pointed the gun at me.

"Oh, give it up," he said, pulling the trigger.

The bullet struck me in the chest, slamming me against the shelf. Had it been a few inches to the left, it would've gone through my heart. The taste of blood filled my mouth, and the feeling rushed out of my legs. I moved my hand around helplessly, still trying to push myself up, knowing only that I had to save my kids, knowing that I didn't stand a chance.

My palm poked against Gaggles' teeth, drawing blood.

"I'll see you in a bit," said Farley. "I'll be the one with your children's bloody corpses slung over his shoulder."

He walked over to the doorway.

"Farley..." I croaked.

He turned around. "Do I have to shoot you again?"

I was seriously injured, maybe even dying. I had only one chance to save Theresa and Kyle. Nothing mattered, not the pain, not the blood, not the fear...nothing but doing what I had to do. And with a shriek of agony as my arm felt like it was being wrenched from its socket, I flung the skull at Farley.

Gaggles' open mouth struck him perfectly—upper jaw through the chin, lower jaw through the neck. The cowboy hat stayed in place.

Farley stiffened.

Let out a gurgling sound.

Then fell.

My last bit of strength was gone. I couldn't even call out my children's names. I closed my eyes and hoped for the best.

* * *

"Andrew? Can you hear me?"

I opened my eyes. Either Bruce or his twin brother Tony was crouched in front of me.

"An ambulance is on its way," Bruce or Tony said. "You don't have to worry about your children. They're safe with Tony. They're badly shaken, but they're not hurt."

"How'd you..."

"Find you? We followed you. We weren't just going to let you waltz away from the police station without surveillance. You lost us for a bit, but the explosion led us right to you. Sorry about the fib."

"Asshole," I whispered.

Bruce smiled. "You just relax. Everything is going to be fine."

"Maybe...but...not after..."

"Shhhh. No need to talk."

"...not after...my wife finds out..."

EPILOGUE

If Helen was pissed, she didn't show it. I'd never been babied so much in my life.

Michael hadn't been bluffing about having to make a call by Friday. By Saturday the names of everyone involved in the snuff videos, from kidnappers to clients, had been made public. It only took about two weeks for the last of them to be caught.

Roger doesn't throw a Frisbee as well as he used to, but after a nice long hospital stay he was all right. My hospital stay was even longer, but I healed pretty well, too. Helen's broken leg did just fine.

Theresa and Kyle...well, there were a lot of nightmares at first, but they're subsiding. It's been six months now, and I think they're both doing extremely well considering what happened. Their psychiatrist is one of the biggest nerds imaginable, but he's good. And kids are tough. They'll be okay.

They say that any publicity is good as long as they spell your name right, but the crew disbanded Ghoulish Delights anyway. Rachel became something of a hero for rescuing the prisoners, but I think she squandered her fame on getting more people to buy gym memberships.

Reverse Snowflake has a nice home now. Roger has a few new scratches every time I see him, but he'll live.

Now I've been offered a generous amount of money to tell

my story. I have to admit, there was some hesitation on my part. I mean, that's what Farley wanted. The problem is, his story got out to the public anyway, even with all the interviews I refused to grant. The former prisoners shared everything, and Farley's final tape (which miraculously survived my blowing up a large percentage of his cabin) seemed to be on television twenty-four hours a day. He got what he wanted.

But, what the hell? Here's my book. Here's a nice summer home for myself and Helen, and a college education for Theresa and Kyle. And I paid off the guy whose car I hit...though, unfortunately, Helen found out about it.

Yeah, this is what Farley wanted, but you know what? He's dead, and I'm not.

I may suck as a detective, but right now I feel pretty good.

In addition to **Graverobbers Wanted (No Experience Necessary)**, Jeff Strand is the author of such twisted novels as **Mandibles, Single White Psychopath Seeks Same**, **Casket For Sale (Only Used Once), How to Rescue a Dead Princess**, and even a book for kids (and adults who were warped as kids), **Elrod McBugle on the Loose**.

You can visit his Seriously Whacked website at www.jeffstrand.com or subscribe to his ridiculous but free newsletter by sending an e-mail to seriouslywhacked-subscribe@yahoogroups.com.

He lives in Tampa, Florida.

Mundania Press LLC

www . mundania . com
books @ mundania . com

No Mercy! No Escape! No Picnic!

The demented mind behind Graverobbers
Wanted (No Experience Necessary), Single
White Psychopath Seeks Same, and Casket For Sale (Only Used Once) is back with
another outrageous blend of the humor-
ous and the horrific.

Extremely large and vicious red fire ants
(Solenopsis invicta) are on the loose in
Tampa, Florida, and those who don't immediately become ant chow must figure
out how to stop this attack before the entire city becomes
overrun by the creatures. Whether you love ants, hate ants,
or have no real opinion of them as long as they're not currently stinging you, you'll love this over-the-top, action-
packed, tongue-in-cheek insects-on-the-rampage thriller!

Hardcover . ISBN: 1-59426-005-2
Trade Paperback . ISBN: 1-59426-006-0

The Andrew Mayhem Series
by Jeff Strand

Graverobbers Wanted
(No Experience Necessary)

When you're desperate for money, searching for a little adventure, and aren't the most responsible person in the world, you can end up doing some outrageous things. Which is how Andrew Mayhem, an extremely married father of two, ends up accepting $20,000 to find a key ... a key buried with a body in a shallow grave. When the body turns out to not only be still alive, but armed and dangerous, he realizes that he should have held out for more money.

Trade Paperback • ISBN 1-59426-348-5
Hardcover • ISBN 1-59426-012-5

Single White Psychopath
Seeks Same

"Sometimes you wake up in the morning and you just know it's going to be the kind of day where you end up tied to a chair in a filthy garage while a pair of tooth-deprived lunatics torment you with a chainsaw. So as I struggled against the ropes, I can't say I was all that surprised."

Trade Paperback • ISBN 1-59426-349-3
Hardcover • ISBN 1-59426-013-3

Casket For Sale
(Only Used Once)

Unfortunately, when you're Andrew Mayhem, you just can't help being attacked by a group of savage killers bent on inflicting ghastly torture and bringing horrific death. Relentlessly pursued through a booby-trapped forest, it's one crisis after another as Andrew fights to protect his family, loses a body part or two, and faces the single darkest moment of his entire life.

Trade Paperback • ISBN 1-59426-350-7
Hardcover • ISBN 1-59426-086-9

CPSIA information can be obtained at www.ICGtesting.com
Printed in the USA
LVOW061738241112

308656LV00002B/334/A